Freewheeling

Essays on Cycling

ALSO IN THIS SERIES

Freewheeling

Essays on Cycling

DAUNT BOOKS

First published in the United Kingdom in 2025 by
Daunt Books
83 Marylebone High Street
London W1U 4QW

1

A CIP catalogue record for this title
is available from the British Library

ISBN 978-1-917092-06-7

Typeset by Marsha Swan
Printed and bound by TJ Books Limited, Padstow, Cornwall
www.dauntbookspublishing.co.uk

Contents

Cycling with Others

Cycling in the City

Break the Ice (Love Theme from Rad)

IMOGEN BINNIE

It took me a couple decades to figure it out, but I was already trans in 1986. I just didn't know back then that being trans was a thing. All I really knew was shame, and maybe guilt.

This isn't about being trans. I transitioned a long time ago and the last thing I want to talk about is gender. This is about bikes. Although I guess it's about bodies, too.

Almost forty years later, I'm a therapist. I think about bodies a lot.

The film *Rad* came out in 1986. It tells the story of small-town paperboy Cru Jones, a BMX enthusiast whose dream is to race on the epic Helltrack – a prestigious, groundbreaking new kind of race 'that combines the different styles and skills of BMX racers and freestylers'. In order to do so, however, he has to surpass the underhanded trickery of sleazy businessman Duke Best and his minions; win over his mother, who believes strongly that choosing Helltrack over his college entrance exams is a self-destructive choice; and beat the effortless talent and skill of professional BMX rider Bart Taylor, played by 1984 Olympic gymnastics champion Bart Conner.

When *Rad* is remembered by film critics, it is not remembered fondly. It has a green splat from critics on Rotten Tomatoes.

But I was seven. This was the VHS era, and the peak of BMX as a fad. We rented *Rad* over and over. We looked up to Cru, and also to Christian, the female BMX rider who teaches Cru to love (and to do flips).

The kids on my block in the woods of New Jersey all rode BMX bikes. We grew up on quiet streets, with woods to explore, a terrifying stretch of active train tracks, and a big pile of old-fashioned wooden shutters with faded yellow lead paint flaking off them that a neighbour said we could have.

We used those shutters to recreate Helltrack as best we could. We built ramps. You'd put a piece of firewood down at one end, lay the shutter on top of it at an angle, and launch yourself into the air.

I was four feet tall, probably weighed fifty pounds, and jumping six inches into the air from a broken shutter and a hunk of firewood felt like flight. Like freedom. Like power.

Like a body was the best thing in the world you could have.

I'm sure you know about the fight or flight response – the state of alert that our nervous systems go into when threatened. You may or may not be aware that, as time has gone on, two more F's have been added. Now it's fight, flight, freeze and fawn. Fawn is about flattering and caretaking the people around you to keep yourself safe.

I landed on freeze. I got stuck there.

I wasn't abused or anything, but our bodies don't differentiate between Big Trauma and Little Trauma. They just fight. Or fly. Or freeze.

I don't remember a lot from my childhood, but I do remember trying to watch a children's cartoon called *Jem and the Holograms* in secret. If you're not familiar with it, it's about an all-woman New Wave band fronted by a pink-haired singer and the very slightly edgier also all-woman New Wave band who try to kill them.

I didn't have a lot of time to myself at age six. It was difficult to watch cartoons without being noticed. But I did everything I could to absorb whatever brief seconds of that half-hour long, neon-coloured pop-music toy commercial I could. I knew that I wanted to, and I knew that I wasn't supposed to want to. As a kid, I felt this way about pretty much everything – if I wanted something, it was probably not OK to want it, so it wasn't worth acknowledging to myself or anyone else. So I froze.

Except when I was jumping off shutters on an imaginary Helltrack.

Blumhouse made a film adaptation of *Jem and the Holograms* in 2015. Don't believe the green splats on Rotten Tomatoes. It was great.

There was puberty. There was teenage drug abuse, there were romantic relationships I didn't know how to be in because I didn't know how to want anything without freezing up in shame. I kept a lid on it. Physically, if not emotionally, I attended college. Then I moved to New York City.

There were more relationships I didn't know how to be in. Drug abuse evolved into alcohol abuse, just because it was easier. I played in bands because I liked bands, I worked in bookstores because I liked books, but actual, vulnerable desire remained impossible.

My memory of my years in New York is pretty sporadic, but I sort of remember that there was another puberty.

Transition is often framed as the thing you do that solves all your problems – 'then I was finally a woman and I lived happily ever after' – but that framework ignores everything we actually know about trauma, nervous systems, bodies and minds.

I had been white knuckling my whole life, dissociated from the shame I had not yet figured out how to engage with. Transitioning didn't change any of that. Anxiety is in large part a habit, a cycle of thought and action and then thought again. Depression is the same. So is shame. The things we do to make these afflictions bearable, they become habits too. And habits don't just disappear because we want them to.

I don't remember specifics, but at some point I went home to my mom's house for a couple days, and when I came back to New York I brought my old BMX bike with me.

As a therapist, I believe strongly that we all have an innate drive to feel better, to heal. Our trauma histories and habits can co-opt that drive, though: generally, into short-term distress relief. I don't remember why I decided to bring that bike back with me – probably something to do with a memory of feeling cool on it combined with the fact that bike commuting could take money from my scant subway fare budget and put it into my forty-ounce beer bottle budget – but looking back, I think it was that innate drive to heal, to grow, like the weed that somehow pops through the cement of the sidewalk, doing its thing.

I don't remember what happened to that bike, which I must have got as a teen. Maybe it was stolen? The important thing is that soon some friends found me an ancient, heavy, blue twelve-speed.

I have a very clear memory of the first time I rode that bike from Brooklyn to work in Manhattan. I remember carrying it awkwardly down three flights of stairs from my apartment, getting on it and starting slowly, tentative and wobbly, down quiet residential Hart Street. I remember the cold air on my face, the opposite of the muggy heat on the train. I remember feeling like ... Can I just do this? Can I just be out here, in the world, in the air? Can I take up space this way? Can I trust cars not to kill me?

I remember turning, terrified, onto Broadway, one of the big arterial streets.

In that part of Brooklyn, there are bodegas and squat apartment buildings on either side of the street, just like anywhere else, but the subway runs along Broadway above you. Between that bridge and the buildings, there are only a few minutes of the day when the sun makes it to the street. It's kind of depressing. It feels like being inside all day. And I guess I wasn't often there at that point in the morning, because I remember very clearly that the sun was shining down on me through that bright sliver of sky as I waited for the light to change.

I didn't have gloves on. I must have just kept my hands in my pockets when I walked to the train, but outside in the air, I remember that my hands were cold and dry. I remember thinking that I would have to get gloves.

I doubt there were cobblestones, but it felt like there were. The street was awful. I remember how deep the potholes were, far deeper than the potholes anywhere else I'd lived. I remember realising that they would actually matter now, could affect me. I couldn't just ride over or through them. I'd fall, or blow a tyre, or bend a wheel.

I had a deeply unfamiliar sense of vulnerability. I'd spent most of my life safe in an elaborate system of defences against shame, fear and grief. But in this moment a pothole could kill me. Or a bus. Even an unpredictable pedestrian, or anyone so maniacal that they'd drive a car in New York City.

The kind of safety I was used to was about not having a body. Disappearing. But here I couldn't help but take up space. I existed.

I remember that first light changing. I remember being worried about the cars I was riding near, and then being surprised by a corresponding feeling – no, I *do* get to take up space – and an unexpected sense of power.

I don't know if I'd felt power like that before.

I had a body. I was present in it. It could do things.

These cars could watch the fuck out for me.

Riding a bike in New York takes all your attention. You're using your legs, your arms, your shoulders, your core. You're listening, you're watching. You can smell the garbage.

I remember riding up to the Williamsburg Bridge. It looked impossible. I remember not knowing if my legs would be able to get me to the top.

I remember a new, oppositional part of me taking over: I'd will myself up there. It was not about my muscles. It wasn't a question. I'd do this.

I did.

My legs hurt, but I got up to the peak of the bridge. I remember how much wider the East River looked from above. I remember the way the angle of the sun made the waves sparkle. I don't think I'd ever thought about there even being waves in the East River.

I remember being hot inside my wool peacoat, sweaty on the inside and cold on the outside. It's windier up there than it is down on the street.

I remember coasting down the far side of the bridge, proud I'd done it, then waiting for the light at the bottom, in Manhattan, panting. I remember some insane-seeming person not waiting for the light, just swerving full speed into traffic.

I don't remember how many days it would be until I was doing that too. Maybe one.

I remember the long avenues and bike lanes of the Lower East Side looking bland in comparison to the bumpy streets of Brooklyn. I remember feeling like I'd accomplished something as I took the giant chain from my waist – similar to the one Joseph Gordon-Levitt wears in the classic (and splatless) film *Premium Rush* – and locked my bike to a parking meter outside of the bookstore.

I felt good. That was new.

I remember wondering if I would just get to work sweaty from now on.

I would.

Riding a bike got me into my body. I'd commute by bike around New York for a couple years, then move to Oakland, California, where I'd bike up and down the East Bay for a couple years more. They put in a new bridge between Oakland and San Francisco a few years ago, something like seven miles long, and I heard it has a bike lane. If it had existed when I lived there, I would have commuted into band practice on my bike twice a week.

We had an indie punk band. It was all women. I had pink hair.

I learned to trust, and love, at least one person. We got married. I gave up drinking and drugs not out of personal growth but because the hangovers kept getting worse until they weren't worth it. Turns out I fried my thyroid. Whoops.

We moved to the woods of Vermont. We had kids.

I turned forty. Somehow, after that, birthdays continued to happen to me.

I don't remember what happened to that blue twelve-speed. I sort of remember that at some point it was fixed up and donated.

I got a secondhand ten-speed from a guy with a barn full of bikes who called himself 'the bike resurrector'. It's grey. It doesn't feel as good to ride as that blue behemoth, although if I'm being honest, I don't know if anything could.

I don't remember what made me decide to show my seven-year-old and my four-year-old the movie *Rad*, but I did. My seven-year-old appreciated it, but my four-year-old got *really* into it. Immediately after our first screening, she ran to the front door, got on her tiny bike, and rode directly off the edge of the porch onto her face.

I couldn't have been prouder.

She started wearing all red every chance she got, just like Cru does when – stop here and watch *Rad* first if you don't want spoilers – he does manage to race at Helltrack. We have spent a lot of time listening to the power rock soundtrack. When we're able to, we drive forty minutes to the closest thing to Helltrack we have, a dirt pump track with ramps where we could learn to do flips, if we had someone to teach us. And our knees don't hurt.

Turns out they still make BMX bikes. Last summer I bought a red Sunday EX. I am tall and old and I'm sure I look silly riding up and down the street pedalling with my legs all bent, but I don't care. I'm a mom. Nothing I do is going to make me look cool. And nothing gets me out of my head and into my body, into the present, as quickly as getting on a bike in the wind and the sun.

I want to say something wise and profound here about childhood and trauma and embodiment and healing and how, if we're doing it right, we can help our kids be less messed up than we were, but I can't quite find the words. But I think it's OK that I can't find the words that I want here. It's always been safer in my head, where the words are, than it's been in my body, where the feelings are. I'm not even going to make a self-conscious joke about movies and splats or the differences between myself and Cru's mom.

All I want to do right now is ride bikes with my kids. My kids are stoked to ride bikes with me. That's a pretty good place to be. I just wish we had some shutters.

Lime Bike, After a Party

ANNIE LORD

My favourite part of a night out is Lime biking home. Scan the QR code of these electric bikes and the bike makes this satisfying boo-ba-doo-doo-doop noise and then charges you £1 for unlocking it and then 15p a minute of your ride. You will often see their green-and-white frames collapsed on pavements across London or hear the odd click-clack-clacking of one of them hacked by an enterprising teenager. As soon as I've dumped my inappropriately small handbag in the front basket and pushed off down the road, I feel a sense of peace. With the only sound the occasional whoosh of a taxi overtaking me and the sky streaked with raspberry ripple as the sun breaks into the day, I pedal my way home, back to my warm bed.

It says a lot that I love this moment best of all, because I really, really love nights out. I saw a friend the other day and apologised for my husk of a voice, the result of a big night out, but they said they'd never met me when I hadn't sounded like I'd smoked a hundred cigarettes. My whole week is structured around some sort of event at the end of it: I'll make sure I get to the gym at least two times and write enough of my book; in the mornings I drink a greens powder that tastes of mud because an influencer I follow convinced me it would prevent bloating; in the evenings I'll walk around in a collagen-boosting LED mask and run a gua sha along my jaw line to sharpen it. As the week draws on, I work out which outfit I haven't worn in a while, go on Pinterest to see different ways of styling it, and think maybe my cowboy boots will go? Or I could tie a black ribbon around my neck? The night before I'll shave myself all over, even my big toe, I'll fake tan, scrub off the dry skin on my lips with sugar. Sometimes this routine is so disciplined I become a bit of a recluse, only speaking to people when I'm ordering coffee in a café, or when I bump into a flat-mate as we cross paths in the kitchen on a late-night snack mission. But that only makes it all the sweeter when I finally do let go, when I shake my hair loose, scream songs out, chat with someone who I haven't seen in ages, the pair of us bathed in the red glow of an outdoor heater, my voice already cracking in my throat. I'll tell them something funny that happened to me. Like how the other week I was flirting with some guy at a bar and he asked my name and I said, 'guess' (and the friend will laugh because it's such lowest common denominator flirting), and when the guy couldn't get it, I told him that it was Annie and he said, 'wow, that's such a granny name' and it was so strange to learn how other people must perceive my name because no one would ever normally tell you when they don't like your name and you can't determine that yourself because you've heard it too many times. That will lead on to a conversation about how we perceive different things about ourselves, like the fact that how we view our bodies is so dependent on how disciplined we think we've been. For instance, sometimes I hate mine because I feel as though I've eaten badly, lots of chocolate, or a pizza for dinner that I ordered on an app even though the restaurant is three minutes from my house, which is all stupid because, in reality, my body hasn't physically changed at all. And as I'm carrying on to my friend who I haven't seen in ages, nodding wildly, I will feel this fiery thing in my stomach, already knowing the next thing I want to say, my leg bouncing underneath me.

It's my favourite thing in the world, getting a laugh out of people, following a conversation as it turns down strange paths. I want to be around it all the time. I know not everyone is like this. My friend Nik, who's an introvert, was telling me once about this time where he surprised himself by being a lot more social than usual. He was at a festival and getting on with the group so well, staying up late looking at the stars, talking about past loves, that when he had to go back to his tent to grab something, he couldn't believe he was rushing. He wanted to get back out there because he already felt as though he was missing out, whereas normally he would be taking that time to gather himself, take a deep breath, relax before joining back in. Listening to Nik I thought about every time I go to the toilet when I'm out, squeezing my bladder so that I can wee faster, already thinking of things I want to say.

When I make it back into the party I'll bounce around, unable to commit to anything, looking over people's shoulders to see which conversations look funner, louder. I'm thinking about my friends upstairs in a booth with their legs plaited over each other, how I just saw Hannah head outside with Hayley and I want to ask how their night is. When I feel like this, agitated, unsettled, everywhere and nowhere, I drink more to try to calm myself down, taking shots from the plastic hat that sits on top of the cheapest tequila bottle from the corner shop. It helps, I sink into my surroundings, my shoulders roll back into their sockets,

I stop thinking about what I'm going to say before I say it, I slow down. But sometimes in that slowing down I talk without thinking, like the other week when I said to one girl that she looked like, 'a dead Victorian school child, but in a sexy way'. And in and among all this talk there's not much time to process what's really happening, how I really feel. To spread out on the sofa with a friend as she gives me a scalp massage while someone else talks about how their landlord refuses to solve their damp problem. To dance to 'Like a Prayer' very literally, getting on my knees when the song says to, disco lights dotting the walls. To be in the moment, laughing, enjoying myself.

Soon enough it's nearly daylight and it's time to go home and sleep, and I'm riding a Lime bike. I get this strange 'you and me against the world' feeling, as though this machine and I are working together. I'm probably talking to the bike because when I'm drunk and alone I tend to do that, saying 'right, let's get your seat down' and 'OK, good, your light is on' as I scan the bike's barcode with my phone and it blinks awake. And then I'm off into the night, all the pressure to perform, the hosting mode I enter when I'm not hosting, it's all gone because there's no one else, there's just me and this metal horse underneath me. Flecks of mascara on my cheeks, chin pink from where the foundation has worn off, none of it mattering anymore because I can look however I want now, say whatever I want, be as ugly and wild as I feel, because no one will see or hear me; I'm in outer space, floating through the cosmos.

For the first time all night, it's quiet. I rarely allow myself silence. I do everything with background noise: podcasts are the soundtrack to my life, I brush my teeth while an influencer talks about the most famous person who ever DM'd them and I walk to the shop listening to the history of Botox. I need distraction, otherwise countless thoughts slip in – that I might not be able to finish the book I'm writing, that the guy I'm seeing on Thursday is going to cancel, that the world is burning, that our politicians only care about their careers. But I know it's dangerous to put headphones in while cycling, so on my Lime bike, it's finally just me and my thoughts. Sometimes I replay scenarios that make me anxious, like maybe I think of when I told a girl she looked like a dead Victorian school girl but in a sexy way. But mostly it's like I'm inside of the night experiencing it for the first time. Soaking up all the moments that ran past me when I was grounded in them.

I use the Lime bike for nights out because I don't want to cycle there, only back, otherwise: helmet hair. During the daytime, I'm likelier to use my own bike and my thoughts don't tend to bend and spiral, they're not creative; they're usually tied into the routine of the day, what food I should make and then freeze, should I put those brown leather trousers on Depop, why is that chapter not working? In these instances, I take the silence and I twist it into something productive because I still have so much to do and no time to do it, so resting isn't allowed. It's part of the routine and order that I break through every Friday when it's the weekend and I'm meant to unwind.

At night I'll be steering the Lime bike between the houses in Peckham, past all the homes with the nice hedges, through to the strange pink and orange one with eyes painted on it, and then the black one with rainbow lines, everything ghostly and quiet, almost eerie – but a fear it's fun to indulge, spiked with adrenaline. Free to entertain myself, sometimes I imagine that there's a zombie apocalypse and I'm trying to escape the city. I'm the girl from the *Walking Dead* with the sword on her back, riding a horse back to safety, except the horse is a Lime bike.

Because here's another thing: it's scary navigating a city as a woman, much scarier than this, usually. I'm not saying it's safe to get on a Lime bike at the end of a night out, but it certainly feels better than waiting around on dark street corners while Ubers cancel and cars slowly loop past, when people follow you off buses and say, 'It doesn't matter I just want to be friends' when you tell them you have a boyfriend. The choice to get on a bike and ride wherever you want to go is freeing, how I imagine it is for men when they go on a run at night, the purple and red lights of the local Chinese restaurant flashing by; the warm, buttery yellow squares of living-room lights left on.

Cycling home after a night out is one of those rare instances where you stop and take stock of life and really feel how perfect it is. I once read an article describing happiness not as a permanent state that you reach, but as a series of small moments that pass by so quickly, you turn around and they're almost gone. Walking back home from seeing friends, a warm coffee in your hands, putting on a film you really want to watch; the first sip of red wine when it starts to get cold outside; hearing good gossip. And a bike ride home at night, after a party. A small dose of happiness, one that is gone as soon as you acknowledge it. As I ride up a hill, the bike's electrics click, and I feel life intensely. And, for a little while, I'm free.

Four Bike Rides, Four Years in the Life of Black Britain

ANIEFIOK EKPOUDOM

2020

That was the summer we cycled out of celebration. That was the summer we cycled out of resistance. Can you picture it? More than 1,000 of us moving through an empty central London like a flock of birds. There was no hierarchy or dress code. There were racing bikes and there were mountain bikes and there were rented Santander bikes. Men and women. Middle-aged adults, teenagers and children. Almost all of us were Black. We had come from all over the country. We had come by ourselves, or in pairs, or in larger groups, until out of many, came a larger whole. A hybrid family, glittering in multicoloured clothing as if we had passed through a rainbow.

The pandemic was still new. In this time of death and anxiety, some of us turned to two wheels to get by. The first Black Unity Bike Ride, in the summer of 2020, was about more than just cycling or exercise. It was a way to feel close in a time of isolation, an escape from a suffocating period. As the pandemic years passed, the annual ride would become tradition. In a time when it felt as if the boundaries between months and years had dissolved, the Black Unity Bike Ride was a reassuringly permanent point on the calendar. During these years, when Black communities across the UK were, at times, at the centre of these upheavals, the bike ride was always there. In my mind, it became a benchmark, helping me register the different phases of the pandemic and to notice how the upheavals were surfacing in our daily lives. More than that, the ride's existence would become a story in itself, a year-by-year record of a community pulling close during a time of wider hostility and uncertainty. What follows is an account of that unfolding.

The memories of March 2020 are strangely elusive. That time feels both recent and distant. Whenever I attempt to remember it, the picture blurs, as if that part of history is begging to be forgotten.

What I do remember is how death became an everyday presence in our lives. It was there on evenings spent watching officials announcing that a new fraction of the population was no longer with us. It was there in the early reports that those of Black African or Black Caribbean ethnicity were four times more likely to die of Covid-19 than those who were white. It was there on phone calls to family and friends, on social media, in stories of people I knew who had lost a father or a brother or more. A member of the church who had not made it. A rapper who had lost a parent, and then posted a desperate video on social media, tears rolling from his red eyes as he begged people to stay indoors.

Among this chaos was a reckoning. The brutal killings of three unarmed Black people in the US – Ahmed Arbery in February, Breonna Taylor in March, George Floyd in May – became the catalyst for the biggest civil rights movement of our time. The Black Lives Matter movement took root in countries all across the world. In Britain, where the well of Black activism runs generations deep, protests were organised throughout the country: London and Cardiff, Liverpool and Belfast, Manchester and Glasgow, Barnstaple and Basingstoke, Yeovil and Southend-On-Sea. Statues were toppled in Bristol. A crowd of 500 gathered at the Guildhall in

Southampton. Thousands signed a petition to rename Glasgow streets called after slave plantation owners.

After protesting came organising. Inquiries into police brutality broadened into demands for racial equality in education and employment, in the health sector and on the football pitch. In July 2020, Tokunbo Ajasa-Oluwa, the CEO of a social mobility charity, decided to stage a mass bike ride through London in the hope that it would bring a sense of unity and empowerment to the Black community suffering a painful hour. Cycling would be a joyful antidote to the darkness.

The first Black Unity Bike Ride was set for 1 August, the same day as Black Pound Day, a new initiative encouraging people to spend with Black businesses on the first Saturday of every month. The plan was simple: to ride from Walthamstow in north London through to Brixton in the south, with a few pit stops in between. Anybody was free to join.

And so, on a warm summer afternoon, we cycled. My partner and I joined the ride at Angel on the borders of central and north London, our rented bikes melting into the flock. London felt like a city abandoned. We turned from empty street to empty street, seeing shuttered shops and restaurants and pubs. There were few cars and almost no tourists. For long stretches it felt as if it was just us out there, the hum of a thousand whining rubber tyres.

As we progressed, the city began to show signs of life. On the edges of Soho, people had sought sanctuary on the curbs, gathering outside bars that were selling alcohol in plastic cups from their front doors. The groups, predominantly white, were stirred from conversation as we passed, at first seemingly confused by the procession. Then, unexpectedly, they broke into applause and cheers. Slightly further along, by the green on Parliament Square, a small group of protesters carrying placards in support of Donald Trump turned and, on seeing us, screamed 'All lives matter', and that the then US president was 'our saviour'.

A few months earlier I had been here, in Parliament Square, after Floyd's murder. Thousands had gathered, and chants of 'Black Lives Matter' and 'No justice, no peace' rang out into the afternoon air. There was grief for Floyd, resignation that it had come to this – again – and there was hope that this time things could perhaps be different. And there was a feeling of sorrow and anguish that, despite the world as we knew it burning, we had still landed here. Even an apocalypse at our shores provided no safe passage or humanity for a Black person in the street.

Seeing the handful of Trump loyalists jeer our presence was a realisation that the very essence of Blackness, our skin, was politicised. A realisation that Black prompted extremes, that we were so rarely granted the safety of obscurity, that we could not cycle together without an assumed meaning, that in others, our presence stoked applause or fear and anger, with little else in between. George Floyd was a victim of such thinking.

As I cycled, I noticed that we were made up of many smaller fraternities. There were the cycling clubs in professional gear who set the pace at the front. There were groups of friends, or family, or strangers who had fallen into conversation with one another, binding into new packs of their own. There was a self-designated soundperson blasting music from a backpack speaker, a trail of listeners in their wake. For the most part, I followed the music, tailed a woman playing the soft bounce of UK garage, and then moved on to a man blasting Afrobeats. There was rap and dancehall, soca and reggae, the many sounds of Britain's Black communities echoing through the streets.

I felt something out there. In a year where the Notting Hill carnival had been cancelled, where Nigerian 60th birthdays and Jamaican nine-night grieving ceremonies had been scaled down to Zoom, where weddings were delayed and baptism celebrations abandoned, where it felt like a time when we only gathered en masse in agony, for those killed, the ride was a release. Here, on the road, in the absence of our old customs, we had found ourselves again.

This was not a protest, or a march. Many had come here for fun. But somewhere on these empty streets, the ride had taken on new meaning. A Black man driving a bus banged his horn in elation, smiling wide and stretching his arm in salute as we passed. Other Black people nodded, or smiled. When another, slightly younger Black man, saw the parade of bikes, he leaped from his car and beat the air in joy. Near Tottenham Court Road, when moving between packs, the music fading into the distance, I saw a cyclist raise her hand from the wheel and trail her Black fist in the air, a quiet salute for all who had pulled in close during this uncertain time.

2021

In August 2021, we hit the road again. We gathered in similar numbers, but for the second annual Black Unity Bike Ride, things felt different. This time we would ride from Walthamstow into the West End before jerking back east and finishing at Shoreditch Park in Hackney. The weather had changed, too. Rain sprinkled the streets in weak bursts, and ponchos were handed out to the riders at every checkpoint. I still followed the music, trailing after a man with a huge speaker in his backpack, and allowed the sounds of 90s hip-hop to waft over me. But we no longer had London to ourselves.

In the months before the ride, London had started to change. The city was correcting itself. There was a time, in the late stretches of 2020, around the second and third national lockdowns, when I would walk every weekend through a near-empty Oxford Street or Regent Street, the centre of the city dormant as a suburban village. By late spring 2021, restrictions were being lifted. Restaurants began offering al fresco dining. We made do with what we could. London gradually reanimated, growing busier with every passing weekend.

During one of my last weekend walks, I stood outside Nike Town at Oxford Circus and saw people streaming across the road in their thousands, bikes hurtling down the street, people spilling over every inch of pavement. I remember the noise, the underscore of a thousand buzzing conversations and car engines. It felt as if all of London's 9 million population had descended on this spot. The city was overcorrecting, trying to claw back a pre-pandemic version of herself that had been for ever lost. People pushed through the street, pushed strangers aside, pushed away the past eight months to the darkest corners of their minds. A brief history was being erased, a city trying to forget lockdowns and grief and misery and everything that came with the pandemic's first and second waves. But there were things that could not be buried, incidents I struggled to forget.

A year had passed since the arrival of Covid. By now, the 'new normal' formed a part of day-to-day life. Working from home, social distancing and masks had become routine.

Other things were new. By late spring 2021, all adults were eligible for their Covid vaccine. But in pockets of London, vaccine hesitancy was high. I saw it surface in conversations with friends who warned me sternly that standard vaccines take years, sometimes decades, of testing before they are deemed ready. The rapid arrival of the Covid vaccine made them suspicious. I saw it on WhatsApp, in broadcasts passed through African communities, claims that vaccines would change your DNA, that they would place a tracker in your body, that they would be used to sterilise Black people en masse. Many advised diet alterations instead. Some shared claims from a widely circulated yet disproven and ultimately retracted study asserting that the MMR vaccine led to a spike of autism among young Black boys. They worried that this Covid jab may be no different. Others shared historical accounts of racial abuse in the medical industry, such as the Tuskegee syphilis study, where 600 impoverished Black men were – without knowing – experimented on by the US public health service for four decades. The past had bred scepticism and distrust. The history of state racism loomed large.

In exchanges with friends, or in WhatsApp groups or on the social media platform Clubhouse, people spoke about the Windrush scandal. They spoke about the death of Belly Mujinga. About Breonna Taylor and Ahmed Arbery and George Floyd. For some, all good faith had been eroded. The vaccine was a boundary they could not cross.

That Spring, at a Jamaican takeaway shop in south London, I stood in the queue, listening to a tense conversation about the first dose. On hearing the exchange, a middle-aged Black man standing behind me cut in. 'Don't take the vaccine', he said, raising his voice, warning all who were present. 'Those people have never given us nothing good. Nothing.' Then he walked out.

Reports from health officials began to bear out these local encounters. In March 2021, analysis by the Office for National Statistics found that while 90.2% of all over-70s in England had received at least one jab, the figure for Black Africans was 58.8%, the lowest in the country. Black Caribbean people over seventy had the second-lowest rate of take-up.

To stave off Covid, many I knew turned to 'natural methods' – supplements and herbal remedies with alleged immune-boosting and antiviral qualities. There was lemongrass and turmeric tea for anti-inflammatory purposes. There was alkaline water to allegedly balance the pH of the body. There was the fruit soursop to fortify the immune system.

One of the most popular supplements was sea moss, a type of seaweed or algae native to the Atlantic shores of North America, Europe and the islands of the Caribbean. It's claimed that it has beneficial effects on the immune system and heart, on digestive and thyroid function, and even that it nourishes the skin.

Sea moss was everywhere that spring and summer. I saw it sold at local food markets by bakers who placed dried packages of the moss next to their chocolate brownies. I saw it on Instagram, posted by independent sellers who blended the moss into a gel and were now selling it by the tub.

I tried it, too. A friend gave me a package to blend and then spoon into my smoothies and stews. Other times, I would be walking the street or waiting at a bus stop, when somebody would approach, and on seeing my grown-out hair, uncut since the beginning of the pandemic, assumed I was a potential customer. They were carrying sea moss in their rucksacks, ready for purchase.

At a housing estate in north-west London, where Covid rates were among the highest in the country, I was offered sea moss and alkaline water by a middle-aged man. 'It beats cancer and all dem tings there,' he told me, patting my shoulder softly as he spoke. In his other hand was a bottle of beer.

By the time the second Black Unity Bike Ride came around, on Saturday 7 August 2021, the previous year's broad enthusiasm for racial equality felt as if it had waned.

Professional footballers were being booed for taking a knee. The home secretary, Priti Patel had described the protests as 'dreadful', and Downing Street repeatedly refused to confirm whether then prime minister Boris Johnson supported the wider Black Lives Matter movement.

There was a feeling among friends, too, that pledges made across many industries in the heat of 2020 were not being fulfilled, a worry that promises of structural change were being walked back or quietly dropped, that racial equality had been the theme for a season, and now that season was over. To survive, Black people were carving out community spaces of their own.

The bike ride offered me a feeling of freedom that I struggled to find elsewhere. When venues had reopened in July, I had tried revisiting nightclubs, but the closed spaces and the sweat and the heat made me anxious, paranoid that Covid was climbing the walls. I tried festivals, but mass gatherings on this scale still felt somehow unnatural.

I tried football, too. The major communal event that summer was Euro 2020, held over from the previous year. For a month there was the distinct buzz only a big tournament can bring. Every match day, the roads around London were washed with supporters in England jerseys and St George's flags. Collective war cries echoed around the streets. It felt as if the entire country had turned its focus to this one event.

The team became a focus for the tensions of the past year. At two pre-tournament friendlies, sections of England fans had booed when the team took a knee ahead of kick off. The same happened in their opening game at Wembley, against Croatia. Afterwards, Patel called the act of taking a knee 'gesture politics', while Boris Johnson's spokesperson said, 'the prime minister is more focused on action rather than gestures'.

England's run to the final became about more than just football. On the weekend of the quarter-finals, my 29th birthday weekend, I was walking through the teeming streets around London Bridge, feeling part of a shared, national moment, when I heard chants of 'EDL' boom through the noise. I turned and saw a group of men laughing as they sang. The moment stung, a reminder that this was something I could never fully embrace. One of the most diverse squads in English history could not erase what was hidden beneath the surface.

After the final, in which three Black players – Marcus Rashford and Jadon Sancho and Bukayo Saka – had missed their penalties, there was an inevitability about what was coming. I braced for impact. But the force of what followed rocked me. The three players were racially abused across social media. The N-word trended on Twitter. Friends on their way home from bars after the game were harassed. A mural of Rashford in Manchester was vandalised. A man accused of racially abusing the footballer on social media by tweeting 'Pack them bags and get to ya own country', later admitted that his children had benefited from the footballer's activism around free school meals. 'He's absolutely brilliant. He's helped my family and I can't thank him enough,' he would say.

Our sense of belonging here still came with an asterisk, with a wariness about some of our own supposed countrymen. We were on unsteady ground. The line between adulation and anger, a compatriot and somebody to be preyed on as thin and as frivolous as a missed penalty.

The bike ride was where I found a sense of quiet liberation. It was a place where I could exist without conditions. It was a loosening of the shoulders. A pilgrimage of sorts. Even though the roads were busy and wet, we were insulated, surrounded by one another. Here, for the second year, I could find refuge.

We didn't ride in a huge pack like the previous year. Groups were separated throughout the journey, pulled apart by the busy London traffic. At times we were walking the bikes more than we were riding them. Towards the end of the Strand, as the traffic lights turned green, a few metres of open road teased out ahead. The pack began to move forward, eager to ride. Then, a crowd of pedestrians who had missed their green signal, angled to walk out ahead of us, blocking our path. Some of the cyclists, myself included, began to retreat, when a voice from the rear of the pack boomed out.

'Stand firm,' the voice shouted, 'You have to stand firm inna Babylon.'

So we fought for every inch of road, hustling and jockeying for space in a city trying to squeeze us out.

2022

By the summer of 2022, a sense of normality had returned. Most Covid restrictions had been lifted and there hadn't been a national lockdown in over a year. The period stretching from March 2020 to July 2022 felt like one long, unbroken year. The scale of what happened will take a few years, even decades, to grasp, but as we emerged from the worst of it, there was some hope. Seeds that were planted two years earlier, when millions flooded the streets in anti-racism protests, continued to flower.

The third Black Unity Bike Ride was set for Saturday 6 August, aligning again with Black Pound Day. Both, along with a host of other initiatives, had become new fixtures in the lives of Black people across the country. Waiting at the end of the ride, in Brockwell Park, south London, would be a dozen or so Black-owned food vendors curated by Black Eats LDN, a restaurant directory for Black-owned food businesses. Like the bike ride and Black Pound Day, the organisation was founded post-George Floyd. Rage had hardened into something more durable, Black organisations building islands in hostile waters after the shared national energy inevitably subsided into apathy.

The day of the ride was also the 60th anniversary of Jamaican independence. Many of the cyclists came with the country's green, black and gold national flag tied to their waists or hanging from their shoulders. Elsewhere, the dress code was the same as before: the seasoned in cycling gear, the casuals dressed down in summer T-shirts and shorts.

The sun was out. As we cycled, the familiar landmarks came into view, High Holborn down into the Strand, and then into the roads around Parliament Square, where today, the scene was filled with tourists taking pictures by red telephone boxes, with families picnicking on the lawns, with people going about their ordinary business.

London was not as busy as the year before. The overcorrection was over. A new rhythm had settled in. The bike ride, too, seemed mellower than in previous years. As we crossed the river at Westminster Bridge, easing our way into south London, the road seemed to open up even further. By the time we were reaching Brixton we had whole stretches of road to ourselves. The flock thinned, and for the last sweep of the ride I cycled largely alone. I watched the Independence Day parties buzz in beer gardens and saw the barbecues smoking on communal greens of concrete council estates. I floated past churches still carrying Black Lives Matter placards in their windows, and saw an elderly Black man, standing on his steps, smiling with a deep joy as we swept by.

On the road, there were no fists held in the air, no feeling of tension or rebellion or despair, just a casualness as we made our way through. An initiative that had its roots in the tense months of 2020 had evolved into an easy, communal gathering ground.

2023

Maybe that's how things would be from here on out. The fourth ride, in August 2023, shared the same mood. People smiled at us on the road, two Black women waved from the windows of a three-storey building, teenagers popped wheelies, bouncing their bikes to the amapiano and reggae playing out of backpack speakers. When a traffic light flicked from red to green, there was a big cheer and we continued on our path. There was an ease to the afternoon. The heat of the pandemic had passed, leaving something in the afterglow.

On those more relaxed rides, people spoke casually about the Notting Hill carnival returning at the end of the month, about the turnover of prime ministers at No 10, and about Lewis Hamilton being screwed out of the 2021 Formula One Championship. It felt routine. There was a permanence about what we were doing, a feeling that this was something as regular as birthdays or Christmas.

I noticed that the crowds gathering at the rides had changed, too. People had started to bring along more young children and babies. I met a young boy with his dad, who had travelled together from Scotland to be there. At one point, I slipped past a fellow rider, his young children fastened to seats at his rear. I wondered about what Britain will look like for them. About the country they would inherit and the rituals our generations would leave behind. About whether they would remember this time, when people gathered together on bikes, riding for safe passage and shelter, finding community out on the open roads of London.

Cycling Through Time

You Are Here

JON MCGREGOR

You Are Here. You know you're Here, because there's a blue dot on the floor plan. The hospital entrance is busy, and loud, and poorly lit. You're disorientated. There are corridors leading off in several directions. The directions you've been given tell you to go to a lower floor, but it's not obvious where the stairs or the lifts might be. Why are we here again? Are you sure we've got the right day? Haven't we been here before? You study the map. You Are Here.

You're thinking about navigation; about the different techniques we use to navigate through our days. And because you've spent a lot of your life riding a bike, you're thinking in particular about navigation as one of the key pleasures of cycling, or even as the actual function or meaning of riding a bike. About the way that riding a bike will always get you somewhere, and the exhilaration and freedom that comes from knowing just how far that might be. About the way that learning to find your way around follows on so quickly from learning to ride a bike in the first place.

You're thinking about a wider sense of locating yourself in the world. About your experiences of being lost, of losing direction, of becoming uncertain of your place. About the experience of watching someone forget where they've come from, or where they're going. Watching their slow dislocation.

There are many ways of moving between these ideas; of creating a journey from one to the next. You're just not quite sure how to proceed. You're wary of taking a wrong turn, of getting stuck in a cul-de-sac. You're not sure, really, where you're going with all this.

You start where you can only ever get started.

Here.

You Are Here, on your bike, leaving town, seeing how far you can get before you have to turn round and get home in time for tea. You're here in Norfolk, a flattish county on the eastern edge of England with a lot of water, a lot of fields, and a whole nervous system of narrow, winding country lanes. It's 1990. You're fourteen, and the summer evenings are long and wide open. You start venturing far enough beyond town that you lose your sense of direction. You get lost often enough to need to come home and look at a map.

The maps of the territory are blue and green, with the roads marked in red, yellow, and white. At the edge of the map lies the sea. The red roads are the main trunk roads, heavy with lorries and commuter traffic and preferably avoided. The yellow roads are called 'B' roads, but if anything the lighter traffic just makes people drive faster. The white roads are your favourite; single track roads where you can hear yourself think and don't have to keep looking over your shoulder.

You start tracing out possible routes, threading the white roads together as far as you can. You trace your finger through Knettishall and Hopton, towards Crackthorn Corner, and Mellis, and Yaxley, and Eye. You wonder about distances, and shops, and water points. Each time you light out you get a little further afield, and eventually you start thinking you might make it as far as the sea. It's fifty miles each way but you're young and the days are long. You look at the route again. You can't carry the thick ring-bound atlas with you, so you write out all the village names on a scroll of paper and tape it to your handlebars. You pack some sandwiches. You take an emergency ten-pence piece for the phone. You tell your mum you'll be home in time for tea, and when she asks where you're going you just say: *out*.

You Are Here, in a taxi. Your mother asks where you're going, again. This isn't the right way, surely. Is the driver going the long way round, to bump up the fare? You're going to the hospital, you tell her. The fare's already been paid. The driver's just following the satnav, look. You point to the display on the dashboard. The blue dot marking where you are. She looks out of the window. I know this road, she says. Haven't we been here before?

You Are Here, and here, and here. You don't know how fast you're going or how far you've gone, but if you keep turning the pedals you keep getting closer to the sea. You pass through towns you recognise from family car journeys, and villages you don't. You get stuck behind tractors. You see flint-built churches, Second World War pillboxes, redbrick Victorian pumping stations. You see village greens, and pig farms, and endless fields of mustard. You've never been this far from home by yourself. You've never gone this long without having to talk to someone. The sunshine and the breeze and the birdsong and the sheer exhilaration of your body moving through space is giving you a feeling which you will later learn to diminish with talk of endorphins but which right now feels closer to magic. You keep winding the scroll of paper around your handlebars, working your way through the villages on your list. Everything is going well, until it isn't. You are here, but you're not Here. You're not where you thought you would be. You followed the signs to the next village, and the signs pointed you the wrong way.

The signs can't be trusted, it turns out. These are the classic fingerposts: black lettering on a white background, bolted to a pole, confidently proclaiming, 'HARLAXTON 2½', OR 'KNETTISHALL 1¾'. They're remarkably easy to tamper with, a tradition which is said to have started during the war to confuse the Germans but which seems to have become habit-forming. At one junction, you see a signpost so worn out from being rotated that the boards are swinging in the breeze, like a weathervane.

You start adding more detail to your route guides – left at the fork by the water tower, right at the cross-roads by the farm – and at some point that summer you make it all the way to the sea. It was too far but you just couldn't resist it. The destination is the thing that counts. You sit on the beach at Dunwich, eating chips, and realise you'll need your emergency ten pence to call home and tell them you'll be late home for tea.

You call home to say you'll be late. You call home to tell them you're safe. You call home to tell them the news. You call home to check everything's OK. You call home to say you'll be over soon. You call home to ask if she's drunk enough water today. You call home to check up on the meds. You call home to go over the plans for the hospital appointment just one more time. You call home to help her find her phone.

You're not sure where you're going with this.

You Are Here, on Dunwich beach again, with your bike beside you, a quarter of a century later. A thousand other people with their bikes beside them, watching the sun rise over the sea. You've ridden overnight from London, a long steady ride when the only navigation aid you needed was the red tail-lights blinking out in a thin lovely line ahead of you. The whir of free-wheels and the clatter of conversations. The shadows of trees and the moonlight above and the slow rinse of dawn into the morning.

Dunwich was where you came for family holi-days, as a child; that's why you marked it on the map for those first cycling adventures. You can remember running down here to swim before breakfast; you can remember your father building a barbecue on the beach. You can remember, one year, the beach café burning down on the first day of the holiday.

You consider calling home to tell your mother you're here again, but you're not sure she'll be able to place it.

You Are Here, on your bike, on the road, finding new territory, pushing ahead without a clear sense of what's coming next. You live in new places, with new people. You ride on new roads. You're a student, a graduate, an employee. You're self-employed. You're a husband, a homeowner, a parent, a carer, a divorcé, a carer again, a husband again. You keep riding your bike. You ride further, for longer, when you can. Your route planning hasn't changed much since those early Norfolk forays. You still sit up late into the evenings, plotting out routes, still trying to thread together those quiet country lanes in a way that makes sense.

You've said *thread together* already. Perhaps repetition has a role to play in reinforcing narrative. Perhaps we've been here before.

The difficulty, in planning routes, is that those quiet country lanes – the ones with the grass growing up in a strip along the middle, and the birdsong, and the lovely views – are quiet for a reason. The scenic routes are the hardest to follow. There are junctions every half a mile, no line markings, unreliable road signs. It's easy to take several wrong turnings before you realise your mistake, and it's frustrating to have to keep stopping to unfold the map and re-route.

So your route planning is a constant trade-off: between choosing the roads you'll enjoy (light on traffic, heavy on the dip and swoop of single-track lanes that duck between trees and fling you across little stone bridges and past hidden farmhouses) and the routes you can follow without having to keep stopping and turning around.

Because the very essence of cycling, the entire design basis of the two-wheeled bicycle, lies in this perpetual forward motion. A cyclist being someone who, as Michael Donaghy puts it, 'only by moving can balance / only by balancing move.' The suspension of disbelief a child first feels when they learn to ride a bike – the held breath a parent swallows when they first let that child go – is carried forever forwards by the gyroscopic force of the turning wheel. You can stay upright if you just keep moving forwards. You can keep going as long as you don't stop.

And this trade-off in the route planning rarely works out. You can either enjoy the quiet roads for a mile at a time, and put up with the stopping and starting and getting lost; or you can keep moving on the main roads, where every passing car is a gamble and a threat. But you keep planning, and you keep riding, and you keep trying to get the balance right.

And then someone invents GPS.

You come out of the lift and the corridor is dark. This doesn't look right, she says. You look again at the set of directions on the appointment letter. You look around for another map. The blue dot. You Are Here. She takes your arm and lets you lead her down the corridor. The lights come on, one flickering ceiling panel at a time, as you edge your way into the dark.

She shows you old photographs, spread out across the kitchen table like maps. She showed you the same photos a week ago. She's surprised to find them after all this time. She gets the names right and the places wrong and the dates entirely approximate. Or the names wrong and the places right. She needs you to help her navigate. This must be before your brother was born. This would have been after you left home. When did we move to that house? Why wasn't your sister with us then? She picks up the photos one by one, trying to piece together a route. When were you born, again? The signposts are all there, but they've been turned to point the wrong way.

You take a long time to start using GPS, of course. You are, if not an actual Luddite, a habitual late adopter. You are wary of adding technology to the glorious simplicity of a bike ride. You have seen how quickly drivers with satnavs lose all sense of where they actually are in the world. Take the next exit. Re-routing. You have reached your destination. Where are we again?

You're more comfortable with paper maps and carefully annotated route guides, you tell people. You prefer to feel rooted in the real world. You keep saying this until you get lost one time too many. You cave in and buy a GPS device to clip to your handlebar, and your whole cycling world is transformed.

You Are Here. You know you are here, because the blue dot keeps reaffirming it. You know which way you'll be turning well in advance of each junction, and so you never need to stop. You know what each junction will look like, because you've planned your route meticulously on Google Streetview: checking how busy a particular lane might be, how passable a roundabout, how safe a short stretch of main road.

Sometimes, you spend so long checking your route on Google Streetview that by the time you're actually riding down the road you're struck by a familiar feeling of déjà vu. Liberated from the need to think about or remember your route, you're stuck instead with the creeping sensation that you've been there before.

Where was I, again? The brain finds the old ways blocked or congested. Re-routes. Sets out across a muddy field. Tramples down a new desire line. A new neural pathway threaded across a blank space on the map. I remember you wearing a pea-green coat. Your grandmother sewed the buttons on. I should remember. I was there. Tramples down a new desire line. A new neural pathway threaded across a blank space on the map. A new memory pulled from the air. I've been here before. I know I've been here before. The pathway becomes the memory of the telling of the story, even when the story was never quite true. The faint lines on the map are erased and redrawn. Re-routing. Please wait. Where are we going, again.

You Are Here, again. Moving down the long hospital corridor. The lights flickering on ahead of you, the lights flickering off behind. As long as you know your next move, it doesn't matter if you lose track of the full route. What are we doing here, again? Are you sure we've got the right day?

You tell her once more that she has an appointment for an MRI scan. That's right, she says, reaching for the old joke: they're going to check if I've still got a brain. It's the way she tells them. The old ones are the best.

Around the corner a nurse is waiting, clipboard in

hand. Did you find us OK, she wants to know. It's a bit of a maze, this place. You'd be surprised how many people get lost.

Life Spins On

MINA HOLLAND

Gordon the hamster loved his wheel. A good thing, too – he needed the exercise. When we bought him, the man in the pet shop told us that he had escaped almost as soon as he'd arrived and only recently been apprehended somewhere in the shop's dog-food supply. Three weeks he'd been on the loose, living it up, and the result was that though he was still young, he certainly didn't look it. Gordy was, as baby hamsters go, obese, and eleven-year-old me took pity on him, promising him a life of actual hamster food and movement.

And move he did. We could hear the wheel creaking all night long. My parents, the type to prefer good brisk dog walks to treadmills, would laugh about poor Gordy and his monotonous exercise routine.

I had to agree that moving round and round without going anywhere seemed extremely boring, not to mention pointless. Imagine! All that effort without a destination or the pleasure of a changing landscape. I wondered if all this exercise was a mark of a frustration, although hoped that Gordy might be exercising for the love of it.

I didn't think about Gordy the hamster at all, really, for about twenty years – until I started spinning. Otherwise known as indoor cycling, nothing else has converted me quite so intractably to the joy of regular exercise. My relationship with sport had always lacked long-term commitment, but arguably I needed it in my life more than most – as a food and wine writer, I effectively eat and drink for a living. Indoor cycling has been a revelation and I feel a new affinity with Gordy the hamster.

Before I go further, I should state that I was a cyclist before I was a spinner. My friend Laura and I even cycled to Berlin from the Hook of Holland in eleven days, covering 600 miles. Two years later, we made the rather less serious trip from Tours to Angers in the Loire Valley, which involved fewer miles and significantly more Cabernet Franc. My cycling career petered out after that, for reasons which included fear of London drivers, a fatal fault in my faithful old bike's gear set, and having two babies.

While I had done the odd spin class for about a decade before February 2022, it was then that my indoor cycling career shifted up a gear. I bought a Peloton. This was not remotely on-brand for me; I just didn't see myself as the type to be cooped up in a bedroom, sitting on a stationary bike while a Lycra-clad Californian yelled at me to remember my worth as I panted up an artificial hill to the sound of tropical house music. Where was the landscape? Where was the wine?

Peloton, a US-based sports-tech company, launched in 2012 with a stationary bike that has a tablet screen attached to it. Users around the world comprise a community – the eponymous 'peloton' – and I'm sure this is integral to the brand's appeal: the rewards of exercising with a group (camaraderie, competition, cheerleading, accountability) without having to leave the house. When I first heard about Peloton, the idea of having one was preposterously decadent but then the pandemic happened, which turned everything upside down and made for great demand in home exercise solutions. In 2020, Peloton's revenue doubled on the previous year. Owning a stationary bike was relatively democratised not by lower prices but by the shrinking of lives – people weren't spending money on gym memberships, or much else besides – and home workouts became the name of the game. Nonetheless, having a Peloton bike does entail privilege, not just because they aren't cheap (at the time of writing, they start at £1,345, on top of which you then pay £39 per month) but because you also need the space for one. Mine lives in a room emblematic of post-Covid middle-class life: a spare bed with laundry piled upon it, a linen cupboard, a desk for working from home and, yes, my Peloton bike, itself loaded with more laundry when not in use. It faces the window so that even if I'm not actually moving anywhere, I can still admire the seasons changing outside. In the last four months, from my bike saddle, I have watched my garden shapeshift:, rotting leaves have segued into daffodils, then primroses, and now our apple tree has burst into blossom.

I have never in my life exercised so regularly or, after that initial outlay, spent so little on it. I used to have what the author and professor of social work Brené Brown would call an 'intense' rather than 'consistent' approach to sport, which meant either fleeting obsessions (such as my hot yoga era) or forking out on memberships and kit which went unused.

As I know all too well, there is no predicting what turns your health will take; all we can do is look after what we have now. For Gordy the hamster, that meant a plastic wheel attached to the side of his cage, and for me, it's my Peloton. Less literally, of course, it's about controlling what we can today because we don't know what tomorrow will bring and so, for as long as I can, I will get on that bike almost every day.

With Peloton, the bike itself is in many ways only a medium to access the motivational rhetoric and mentorship of its instructors. The likes of which I craved, unknowingly, right around the time I got it. I bought it as a present for myself on my daughter Vida's third birthday: it seemed like the antidote to how dreadful I'd felt in my body since becoming a mother.

It is hard to summarise my start to parenting without sounding glib. I mention it here because I am sure it has been instrumental in my conversion to indoor cycling. Vida was diagnosed with a life-threatening blood disorder at four months old, and then my return to work after a difficult maternity leave dovetailed with the first lockdown. My son Gabriel was born eight months after that, early, because I had a critical case of Covid. By the time Vida turned three, I was operating, shell-shocked, in a vacuum of isolation and medical journals; life ticked to the metronome of giving medicine daily to a toddler, trying to wean an infant from my tired boobs and holding down a job. I lived to serve two creatures I loved to a terrifying degree, but it felt like I'd experienced a paradigm shift. The person I'd been for the thirty-three years before motherhood became a spectre; my mind divorced from a neglected body.

I often catch myself using words like 'conversion' about my Peloton, words that suggest a re-routing, some kind of an awakening. People who find religion are called 'born again' for a reason. Since becoming a parent, I haven't found God, but I have experienced a rebirth about which I feel nothing short of evangelical – if sheepishly so. I feel happier in my body than I have ever been, grateful for what it allows me to do, and I can't tell where physical wellbeing ends and mental health begins. They are one and the same.

It seems no accident that Peloton instructors often employ the language of church in their workouts, often with a Southern Baptist bent, such as 'the test becomes the testimony'. This idea that strife, struggle and hard work become your story resonated with me, as did head instructor Robin Arzón's suggestion that, while cycling up a steep gradient, I 'put something at the top of the hill' to keep in my eyeline and work towards.

I had known all along what that something was: the moment that Vida rings the hospital bell to signal the end of her bone marrow transplant treatment. I had bought the Peloton around the time that we decided to go ahead with this treatment, a procedure that would, if successful, be life changing. But it did also come with significant risks. Freddie and I knew that Gabriel was a stem cell match for his sister; in him, we had the donor, but not, in ourselves, the courage. I am

sure that a combination of endorphins from my spinning and the affirmations from the instructors helped
keep me positive enough to imagine the unimaginable.

'Movement is medicine' is another favourite saying
on the platform, and one to which I subscribe. Even
when living in hospital for six weeks during Vida's
procedure, I accessed the app's running and yoga classes,
where I could be drip fed morsels of self-belief in the
form of pithy proverbs delivered warmly, by instructors who seemed to be speaking to me alone.

Look, it's very clever. And yes, perhaps even a bit
cynical at times − like the endless plugging of lulu-
lemon when the two brands collaborated, or multiple
rides 'coincidentally' playing Alanis Morisette's 'Ironic'
in the space of a week − I really don't care. Riding on
my Peloton has been a kind of therapy at a point in
my life when quiet reflection has felt impossible, but a
physical release has been essential. I know I have to be
OK for my children to be so too; self-care is not selfish.
Sometimes, though, I need someone to remind me of
this. And in my Peloton world, that someone is always
an impossibly attractive fitness influencer, often with a
career embracing both professional sport and model-
ling. It is beyond me how anyone can look as these
women do in a single-shouldered sports bra and gold
tights as they somehow juggle chatting with riders in
the studio while playing to the camera, throwing in

the odd motivational maxim before reminding you
that you survived dial-up internet so you sure as fuck
can survive another breathless 30-second speed push,
all while doing the class themselves, all while barely
breaking a sweat. It's a show put on by talent whose
job it is to make it look easy, while reminding you that
life involves hard work, and that you are worth more
than easy. It is also a reminder of the rightward skew
of American politics, and of how liberal Americans –
for this is what I assume the diverse and progressive-
looking Peloton line-up to be – often spout proverbs
that sound curiously Thatcherite to my ears. Get on
your bike and look for work!

Peloton knows its core user base well. They seem to
be split between the serious fitness folk and millennials
who are nostalgic for their adolescence. I like to think
I fall into both categories, taking every opportunity to
relive my youth on an early-Noughties R&B ride or,
for what I imagine must be a smaller but impassioned
audience, a UK garage one with Hannah Frankson.

The idea of life as a journey is tediously baked into
the popular lexicon, as is the notion that meaning can
be found not in a destination or goal, but in how you
get there. But clichés exist for a reason, don't they?
When my daughter was diagnosed, I was so focused on

curing her, that I couldn't imagine life being peaceful or content until we got there. Since her transplant, she has become independent of blood transfusions and getting to this point has shown me a kind a joy I wouldn't have known without the hardest days.

Whether or not we are moving somewhere – on an actual bicycle to an actual place, to the top of a 'hill' on a stationary bike, or simply spinning round and round like a hamster on a wheel – I have learnt the rewards of committing myself to movement and to the moment. Now that Vida's bone marrow transplant has finished, there are other things at the top of the metaphorical hill. While goals like these might spur me on, I like to think that by now I have learnt just to enjoy where I am and the fact that my body can do this: move, heave breaths, perspire and watch the seasons change.

'Hamster wheel' is a term used unfavourably, often about the monotony of the rat race (poor old rodents seem to feature disproportionately in metaphors about high-octane modern life). We all want to get off the hamster wheel of our busy routines that we feel don't allow us pause. But perhaps it's time to put a positive spin (ha) on this trope?

Gordy lived to be three, decent innings for a hamster. I can't help but feel he had a good approach to life, with all the right ingredients: he enjoyed what he ate (I saw to it that dog food didn't feature); he was loved (by a slightly eccentric eleven year old who admired his independent spirit and identified with his appetite); he slept well (in an empty Marmite jar stuffed with a shredded kitchen towel); and he exercised consistently. As hamsters go, he was bright-eyed, curious, energised and happy for human company. Every day (or night, I suppose, as hamsters are nocturnal) that he woke up, he lived fully. Until he didn't. I buried him in his Marmite jar at the bottom of a different garden from the one my Peloton bike looks out over now, but I think of him often while I ride. The world keeps on spinning, and so do I.

The Gasp

ASHLEIGH YOUNG

My cycle commute most days is short but hilly. I dip down a steep treacherous road called Mt Pleasant, where cars often have near-head-ons due to speeding round the blind corners. After that I shoot out onto a hill called Raroa Road and begin the climb towards Kelburn, where I work as an editor. Raroa is a bad road for cyclists – busy and narrow, with a wind that is sometimes so strong it feels like you're riding through randomly thrown pillows or boxes. While riding up this hill, I have cried, flailed my arms at close-passing vehicles, felt dread at the coming day. A couple of times I have accidentally ridden directly over a dead rat, or been swooped upon by a kākā – a chicken-sized native parrot that is abundant in the sanctuary nearby.

But on better rides, maybe if I set off at a less busy time of day, I've felt almost grateful for the hill, as if the effort is scrubbing me clean. From late autumn the air is still, the sky a well-blended eyeshadow, and maybe someone is running along with a dog, or a high-school boy on a scooter yells and raises his fist while speeding down the other way. Even though I'm slogging uphill, I feel like a wide-open butterfly net, catching glimpses of bright, rushing things.

A while ago I got side-swiped by a car pulling out of a driveway. It was a slow side-swipe, but my right foot was briefly caught on the car's front tyre and my shoe and sock were pulled off and flung across the road like a weird firework. The driver still hadn't seen me or my bike – he was in a different, more dignified world in there, gliding forth, with both shoes and socks on. I pushed my bike with its dented front-mudguard onto the footpath, and the driver finally stopped. He wound down his window and uttered the ancient words: 'Sorry, I didn't see you.'

I burbled something at him, then went out to retrieve my sock and shoe. I thought I must look crazy. It was me who was in the different world, I realised, out here with my sweat-wicking layer, my little red rear light, my racing heart, my bare foot. I waved the driver on. Then I put my sock and shoe back on, hopped back on the bike, and wobbled up the hill.

Something happens after a close scrape. Your feelings rise to the surface and seem to blaze so brightly that it feels everyone must be able to see them. There is the fright of being reminded that the barrier between life and death is thin; you feel the full potential and danger of every pedal stroke. For me, the other feeling is a bitter, almost teenage righteousness – with a sting of shame – of being a cyclist in a world of drivers.

Around the time of the sock and shoe incident, I realised I'd been feeling unusually emotional on my rides. I was quicker to gasp, to panic, to anger. If a car passed me too closely, I was all, 'You cunt!' – a new swear word, for me, but the only one that satisfied, though in that double-edged way in which the satisfaction only pours oil on the rage. When a truck brushed me at the traffic lights, I rode faster than I ever had in my life to catch up with it at the next set of lights, where I pounded on its window and bellowed at the frightened-looking old man inside. If a company vehicle cut me off, I googled the company and wrote a polite yet vicious email. I wasn't yet at the stage of wearing a hi-vis vest with 'DAUGHTER' or 'AUNTY' emblazoned on it, but I wasn't far away.

At the end of 2022 I decided I'd start writing a weekly blog about my bike rides. I thought it would help me claw back something of what I liked about cycling. A quiet road, a slow, generous overtake, the feeling of being cold then warming up. And there was something else, with the blog: I wanted to hold on to the time that was slipping away from me. This ordinary time, where I rode the same route, day after day. How could I make something out of it? I thought of Annie Dillard's terrifying line, 'How we spend our days is, of course, how we spend our lives. What we do with this hour, and that one, is what we are doing.' What I was doing with my life: riding the same roads to and from a job that, increasingly, felt like trying to cycle up a waterfall or a hydroelectric dam. Each day, cycling showed me a small bit of freedom but never enough. Brought me a little closer to myself but never close enough to understand why I was so unhappy. Each day I would set sail and something would come loose in my brain, like a pannier strap flapping dangerously over the back wheel.

My mum tried to teach me to drive in her Toyota Nissan when I was sixteen. The lessons didn't take. I was scared of being in charge of the car and maybe killing someone, and scared of my mother's fear, which I could feel when she jammed her feet into the footwell. Her high-pitched gasp – the sound that my brothers and I refer to now as 'The Gasp' – chilled me when I sailed through intersections, and her shriek, when I braked suddenly to avoid an animal that turned out to be a puddle, made me want to throw myself out of the vehicle. She was right to be afraid, I suppose.

We were driving in Te Kūiti, a small town that I should have wanted to escape at all costs, but I had the feeling that cars were for people who were more evolved than me. What business did I have here, trying to drive one? People who drove could fit towns, cities and motorways into their brains all at once; they had an easy, adult fearlessness as they went through the world. When the kids my age started getting their licences, they left the rest of us behind. Especially the boys. Their eyes narrowed, their laugh hardened, the way they gelled their hair became somehow more intentional, more thoughtful. Even though a boy with a driving licence still had long thin legs, even though he still wore the green nylon trackpants of our uniform and still carried a backpack heavy with School Cert textbooks, his walk became the self-possessed walk of a family man, keys a-jangle in his pocket, on the way back to his parked car.

A family friend, Mr Lamb, came round for dinner once and asked us how the driving lessons were going. Mr Lamb was also my high-school English teacher and a colleague of my mother's, who was also my Japanese teacher. Mr Lamb had a car. He had driven cars in England, Australia, and – unbelievably – on the other side of the road, in America. I pictured him driving through the lonely desert – for some reason always the lonely desert – with his sunglasses on, heading for Las Vegas.

'There was a car coming at the Rora Street intersection and she sailed out and nearly hit it,' Mum cried.

'I didn't see it,' I cried back.

'What, you mean you didn't see that big hearse?' Mr Lamb said.

Mum made a soft whistling 'Ssssss' noise – her noise when she wasn't sure whether to laugh at something outright. I asked her what 'Ssssss' meant, once, and she said it meant 'Be careful.' This only deepened the mystery.

For days after Mr Lamb's hearse joke, a scene kept playing out in my head. There was the shining hearse, ferrying the body of some much-respected figure of the town – maybe my music teacher Mrs Archibald, or the town priest, or perhaps Mr Lamb himself – and me at the wheel of the Toyota Nissan. Trying desperately to be careful, I would still manage to drive with full force into the hearse. I knew nothing about cars but somehow I knew that this manoeuvre was called 'T-boning'. During the T-boning, I was seeing the hearse but not seeing it, I was braking but accelerating, I was alert but utterly unconscious, I was leaping out of the car apologising while also curling into a foetal position in the footwell. As time slowed and shattered into pieces, it was clear that everyone except me was dead. The much-respected figure of the town would not make it to their own funeral. Then the scene began again. Later I would learn that this was called 'rumination'.

A couple of years earlier, my fourth-form English teacher, a truly kind and gentle man who walked with a slight bounce – and who looked a bit like Jesus and so was called 'Jesus' by my classmates – had been killed in a head-on collision on a highway not far from our town. His fiancée died with him. Another teacher, from the primary school, had been killed in a similar collision at an intersection near the Waitomo fruit-orchard. And there was the story of my high-school form-room teacher, who as a young man had accidentally hit and killed a small boy who'd run out onto the street we lived on. I was especially shaken by these deaths because they involved teachers, my mother's friends and colleagues.

Even if you were a good driver, like Mr Lamb was, unspeakable things still happened. Recently my brother JP, three years older than me, had been driving his little Cortina at night along a farm road, somewhere between our town and the aero club. All of a sudden, blazing up in the headlights, there were cows. Cows, wandering all over the road, as if it were some kind of street festival. JP braked hard but still drove right into them. He told us about his shock, and the poor cows at the mercy of some carelessly left-open gate. The dark road, and no one else around. How he had run for help to a nearby house, and how a farmer came with a gun.

And there was the turkey. When I was much younger, we were all in the car on the way back from Mōkau Beach. My father was driving, my mother was in the passenger seat, and me and JP and my other brother, Neil, were in the back. It was hot, the paddocks yellowish brown and the rivers low. From a nearby verge a turkey waddled onto the road. I didn't see it, only heard my mother's gasp as my father accelerated. He had a way of accelerating – very suddenly, as though the car were pulling away from underneath you, wanting to be rid of its passengers – which terrified me, and this time was no different. There was a strange thud. I looked out the rear window and saw the turkey tumbling away behind us, a small and terrible explosion of feathers and dust. 'It was it or us,' Dad exclaimed as my brothers and I screamed.

And then the drive simply went on, my father speeding down State Highway 3, through the grey-green farmland towards home. My mother and brothers must have asked him why he had done it, but I remember nothing of his reply, only that he seemed unmoved. My brothers remember looking at the grille of the car once we were home and seeing that it was shattered.

The heartache I felt over the turkey's death was the wrong thing to feel. It was only a turkey. A wild turkey, or maybe a farm turkey, in the wrong place at the wrong time.

I couldn't sleep that night. I was thinking about the turkey. I took 'It was it or us' as a statement of pure bloodthirstiness – there seemed something socio-pathic in it, even – rather than that Dad, in his own way in that split second, had meant to avoid causing an accident on the winding road. That since he believed he would hit the bird anyway, he'd sped up as an act of mercy. But he would never explain this to us. The conclusion I drew was that driving brought out some-thing monstrous in a person. That whatever it brought out, whatever harm it caused in the world, you had to bear silently, speeding onward, because this was what being a grown-up was.

After one too many near misses at intersections, my driving lessons with Mum petered out. My brothers had managed to get their full licences, so they drove me around, and when they left home, I either walked or didn't go anywhere. After I left home and moved to Wellington for university, the idea of learning to drive became even more distant. I would become a person who rode a bike, I decided, mostly so that I could continue to avoid learning to drive, though I soon realised that this was a very elaborate sort of avoidance, like a short cut that takes you into the wilderness or directly into the sea. I also wanted to ride because my brother Neil had moved to London and cycled everywhere – I loved the romance of this, the worldliness – and because one of my writing heroes, the New Zealand poet James Brown, had written a lot of poems about cycling, mostly the pain of cycling uphill. Also, if I were in a crash, the person most likely to be killed or maimed was me, and this simply felt like less hassle.

And now I have been cycling for more than twenty years and whenever I think about learning to drive I am embarrassed to say I still think about the turkey, and all of the other casualties and terrible collisions on those farm roads, the black tyre marks long since faded, so many tiny animal bodies long since turned to dust, so many people gone – and none of that at all out of the ordinary, just that for some reason I wasn't able to bear it.

The punishing hills. The freezing, rain-studded headwinds that could blast the contact lenses out of your eyes. It was Wellington, around 2006, when I first started cycling, and it seemed to be always winter. Drivers were impatient, sometimes indignant, and one time a taxi drove into my leg. There was a period of a few months when teenage boys kept sticking their heads out of car windows and barking like dogs – and here, always, I would do 'The Gasp', exactly like my mother. Happily, my first bike was stolen. But I soon realised I couldn't do without it, the buses being unreliable, so I got another one and started riding around miserably again.

'I could never cycle in the city,' a number of people said to me. 'It must be terrifying.' You're crazy, they meant. But it wasn't that I wasn't scared, or crazy. I was. Riding a bike felt like being a teenager still, out in the open with my feelings, always worrying what the next moment might deliver, always feeling the ache of self-consciousness.

Over time, though, cycling in Wellington and then London and then back in Wellington, my confidence grew, and the feeling of precarity lessened, though I still gasped easily when I got a fright – a flung-open door, a too-close pass, a driver careening through a stop sign as I myself had once careened.

I'd started cycling out of driving avoidance, but I began to like a lot of things about it. Mostly, I liked how the present moment seemed to balloon, especially at night, especially in the rain and wind on my ride home around the bays, as water was torn from the waves and flung over the road. On a bike, at night, the present held more. I felt somehow protected by its bigness. Drivers moved through that same night differently. Without struggling or grimacing, they could leave themselves behind and race into the future.

The blog I began in 2022 traced my rides to and from work, around town, and an occasional Big Ride, when I might go around the bays in the early morning or ride up to the radome, the structure that perched eerily on top of Hawkin's Hill like a huge eyeball. In the beginning, I had a rule that the blog shouldn't voice any feelings I'd had on that day's rides. Focusing on the journey would keep my gaze turned outward. My other rule was that the blog should avoid whimsy at all costs. I didn't want any plastic bags billowing playfully this way and that, no meditations on daffodils jabbing upwards from the earth in spring, no rhapsodising about the bicycle's perfect encapsulation of form and function.

The no-feelings rule fell over almost immediately. In the second week, I wrote about being sent into a weird rage by the sight of a man doing wheelies on a mountain bike. Later that same week, I noted the solar-plexus-joy of speeding downhill. The next week, a ride at night took an existential turn as I became aware that I was 'very small on a dark road'. Then I wrote of my sorrow remembering the sight of a tabby cat that had been hit by a car and left in the gutter next to a construction site; I thought of the cat whenever I passed that place.

It was too hard not to write about such things. When I got on my bike, my feelings found their shape, like a jacket puffed up with wind; anything I had tried to pack down during the day billowed out dramatically. The quivery breaths I took while riding down a hill towards a talk I had to give, and the usual savage post-mortem during the steep ride home. The way I would find myself promising that this was the year, this was the year I would do at least some of the things I was afraid of. Or the way I would be assailed with grief for a friend who had died – I would feel her everywhere, in trees and stars and houses that glowed out of the dark hills on a night ride.

On a bike ride, anything I had been trying to avoid became almost painfully present, as if emboldened by me being alone.

And though I tried to resist the cliché of finding the extraordinary in the ordinary, there was some-thing about looking for things to describe on my rides that almost insisted upon it. I couldn't not notice a pair of blue underpants on the road and be thrilled by them. I couldn't not enjoy riding over a leek, or seeing a woman wearily waving a stick at someone over the road, or passing through a long cloud of weed.

Or by trying to categorise different sorts of rain, even if this brought me dangerously close to breaking the no-whimsy rule.

My only real break in routine was taking the ferry across to Picton and then cycling the treacherous 28 kilometres from the ferry terminal and down to Blenheim, where my parents now lived. The ride was uneventful except for a moment when, riding on the shoulder, loads of tiny apple-like objects appeared – crab apples? – and my tyres wobbled about like a cartoon villain on marbles. And then, a couple of days later, when I was about to set off back to Picton, my tyres sank into the deep gravel in my parents' driveway so I was unable to move, and my mother shrieked in dismay.

In week fifty, after another week of my routine observations and bellyaching about my sore leg, a reader cried in the comments: 'Please write about something else!'

I felt belligerent. Then realised that she had a point.

These were the same roads, and they weren't nothing – but there were other roads.

My mother came to visit me for a couple of days one week. On the morning she was due to catch the ferry home, I walked her down a winding mossy path and a series of precarious steps towards the bus stop. I had my bike, which I sometimes lifted onto my shoulder, and she was walking with tiny, uncertain steps, dragging her purple suitcase behind her, its wheels struggling over the rough ground. Walking with her, I was aware of the steps slippery with moss, the broken bits of path, the steep drop on one side. I kept waiting for something bad to happen – for Mum to gasp and keel over, as she had before on uneven ground. But she didn't. From time to time she would stop and cling to a wall or a rail, and look out over the dark green valley below us. 'Gosh,' she said, 'this view. It's like flying.' She would say this whenever we were above sea level.

This habit of pausing and exclaiming used to make me impatient. Mum would do things like hold up a glass of wine to the light and say, 'This colour! It looks like a South Island river.' Or hold up a plate: 'Look at this. A very French blue.' Nothing could happen until somebody either agreed or scoffed. But as we made our way down to the bus stop, pausing often to look at things, my impatience was gone. Mum's exclamations felt like necessary stops for gathering ourselves – before proceeding on with slightly more courage.

I think it was then that I decided I was going to learn to drive. Although I would always ride my bike, and although I would always be fearful, I wanted to be able to drive my mother to the ferry, or collect her from the airport. I wasn't speaking to my father at this time, but maybe one day we would fix things, I thought, and I would be able to drive him around too. I was forty years old.

Slow Puncture

MOYA LOTHIAN-MCLEAN

My bike starts to fail me in the middle of the Camberwell highway. It's not really a highway at all, that's just how I refer to it in my head. Its modern name is Camberwell New Road and it is a lengthy, pockmarked stretch of thoroughfare that knits together my bit of southeast London and the centre of the city. Google says it's the longest Georgian road in England. They used to hang people at the intersection where it stops being Camberwell New Road and splits off into tributaries, funnelling travellers to different corners of the capital. Usually, this route is an easy one that requires little exertion. But today I'm huffing and puffing. The struggle is exacerbated by the presence – or rather, absence – of my new housemate, who has sped effortlessly ahead of me on her road bike. My own wheels feel as if they have cement in them; perhaps I have a flat tyre. But when I finally reach our destination and gently check the firmness of my wheels, they are not deflated. True, there's slightly more give in the front tyre but it's barely perceptible.

'Maybe it's your bike's weight,' my housemate suggests later, at home. Her sleek white-and-green number is elegant, efficient and slim, much like herself. Mine is a sturdy turquoise hybrid bike, short, squat and dependable. Bikes are like dogs, mirroring their owners.

'Maybe'.

My bike's weight has never bothered me before. It's fairly new, bought full price as an 'adult invest-ment'. My previous bike was an introductory vehicle, a present from the ex-boyfriend who gently coaxed me into becoming a London cyclist. It too was a shade of blue, a bright azure, a 1980s Halfords Freewheeler model in a permanent state of disrepair, with only three working gears. I adored its dysfunction and the fact that I was in and out of my local bike repair shop so much that the staff started giving me discounts and asking me questions like 'what are you all dressed up for?' But finally the chain snapped and the technician who dealt with me most frequently told me to let go; the bike was too costly to keep patching up. Enter the new model. I scrapped my old bike London-style, leaving it unlocked outside overnight. The next morning it had been spirited away. The boyfriend followed suit a few months later. My housemate is still trying to solve the problem.

'Maybe it's a slow puncture?'

A puncture, slow or not, is something I cannot fix. In fact, a puncture is one of the many things my ex-boyfriend used to fix for me. Now I have two options: go to the bike shop for a professional diagnosis or open up YouTube and teach myself a new skill. Based on past precedent, the latter option promises disaster. The bike shop is the sensible option but I am not a sensible person, I am a busy one. I'll go when I have time, I tell myself, knowing I will never have time.

So I let the problem persist – at least in my head. On my bi-weekly ride to the office, I obsessively glance down at the front wheel as it spins along the road. Is it my imagination or is the spread of rubber flatter? Often I will pull over and dismount, compelled to test the density of the tyre. It feels fine.

But the sensation of total freedom when cycling is gone. I am back among the mortals. Every cycle is through treacle, a slog no matter whether I'm pedalling against an upward gradient or not. I start to consider explanations other than my slow puncture. Perhaps it is my body that's failing. I am twenty-eight, a baby in the grand scheme of things, but I have started noticing my body keeping a score it didn't seem to just a few years previously. This is most apparent when I'm riding my bike. At regular intervals, I have to consciously tell myself to breathe, to relax my tense muscles, to stop pressing my tongue nervously against my teeth in such a way that gives me a constant low-level headache.

There are new pains: in my neck, my lower back, my stiff hamstrings. Ever since a weekend spent stomping around Glastonbury festival in platform boots, I've been dogged by a persistent stabbing feeling in the two smallest toes on my left foot. I suspect the pinky is broken – I vaguely recall a kitchen party conversation where someone told me this happens about four times a year. Maybe it will heal independently. In the meantime, I try to ignore the discomfort by wearing wide-fit, comfortable shoes that won't squeeze the toes together. This works most of the time, except when I'm pedalling.

I don't want to dive too deeply into the hows and whys of these new pains, scared of what I'll find. Every person with even a drop of Jamaican heritage knows the story of Bob Marley, felled at thirty-six by melanoma that appeared first under his toenail. Cancer runs in my family: my paternal grandmother died of a lump in her breast, long before I was born. Then her son, my absent father, succumbed to lung cancer when I was ten. When I was younger, his disease felt unrelated to me. Instead of a genetic tendency that could be passed on, it was a special punishment he was served with. As a teenager, I remember telling people something my mother said: that my father's cancer was a manifestation of his badness, eating him up from the inside, as he was a non-smoker. But when I pick over my recollections as an adult, I can't remember her saying that, or even imagine it. She has always been so generous to his memory, fair and pragmatic. 'Badness' is a word inflected with childish resentment. Did I put words in her mouth, to give the opinion a stamp of legitimacy?

Now, my father's cancer, and the cancers of his ancestors, feel like my problem. I am haunted by the constant certainty that the rotten cells are mutating and proliferating inside me, despite a complete lack of symptoms that would suggest this is happening. I fixate on a small, ugly raised growth on the outside of my wrist as a likely site for the illness to make itself known. The lump looks like a wart but it won't go away, even with repeated applications of the requisite treatment. I try to cut it off with nail scissors, the way I have with warts in the past. The wound bleeds and bleeds and bleeds but when the blood congeals enough to gently mop up, I see the DIY operation has barely removed any of the offending tissue. It is almost certainly a wart. But still. I keep intermittently pruning pieces off, dropping bloody flesh confetti into my bedroom bin. I pump up my outer bike tyre even though it's the inner tube where I suspect the trouble lies. I do not book a doctor's appointment and I do not visit the bike shop and I do not consider why these things seem beyond my capabilities.

Instead, I keep riding my bike and thinking circular thoughts, every time I look at my maybe-a-bit-flat tyre, about my health and who could solve the problems I can't. My stepdad would be able to mend a slow puncture in seconds. He is a self-taught mechanic, architect and builder. When I was younger, he could fix anything, from the back wall of our house after the living room was flooded one wet winter, to paying for new pairs of shoes and school uniforms when my mum's benefits didn't stretch so far. My first bike – a child-pleasing turquoise – was a gift from him. I remember learning to ride it on the drive outside his house, which he had paved himself. 'Go on,' he would say gruffly, setting me and my sister off to peddle, peddle, peddle as fast as our little legs could go.

Legally this man is not my stepdad because he is not married to my mother and has never lived in the same house as us. But since I was five years old, he has served as my father figure, so 'stepdad' somehow fits. Our love language has never been emotional; he speaks in gifts and money. Throughout childhood, this looked like funding for school trips, new shoes and holidays to Cornwall, things my single mother could never have afforded solo. As an adult, the nature of these presents has changed. Recently, I proudly told my stepdad how I had paid for my new bike myself. A few days later, a cheque arrived, bearing the same figure and his signature.

But in recent years, he has slowly begun opening up emotionally, a process older men seem to embark on as they inch closer to the end of their time on earth. My stepdad suddenly wants to talk, mainly about dying. He couches these discussions in practical terms: the music he wants played at his funeral, the coffin he's ordering, who will execute the will. Yet they are underpinned by a familiar terror: will I be missed? Do you love me enough to see I am mourned? Our main form of communication is usually one-way, via jaunty little postcards that I send every few weeks, but on the rare occasions I return home, I am treated to a litany of worries wrapped up as rational preparation. These always take place over an expensive lunch, often with him slipping me another cheque when he's driving me home, still trying to buy the love he already has for free. When I was little, he used to joke about 'cupboard love', saying we only wanted him around when he bought us things. I thought this was a joke about childhood greed. I now see it was an adult fear that had precisely nothing to do with Tangfastics.

At Christmas, I host my mother and sister in London; our first time spending the holiday away from our countryside home in twenty-three years. It is also our first without my stepdad because he and my mother have fallen out, after twenty years together, over money. At midday, I get a call – it's him. We don't often talk on the phone. He's bored, he says. The brother he is supposed to be spending Christmas with is sick. I realise he is alone and try not to betray my sadness; he would read it as pity. Instead, I thank him for the cheque he gifted me.

One morning in January, I wake up and discover a constellation of angry red pustules on my chin. Over the following days, they creep like ivy, across my cheeks, up my temple and in the T-zone between my nose and eyes. At first, I decide this is the result of the new Korean skincare routine I have been trialling. But the acne won't clear and when I spot blood on toilet tissue for the first time in three years, I remember my contraceptive implant and try to recall when I last had it replaced. Usually I measure this via boyfriends. But that metric is gone, for the first time in years.

I get on my bike and race to the nearest sexual health clinic; they don't have any walk-in appointments free. I hop back on my bike, riding it to the next-closest clinic, twenty minutes away. They can fit me in for an implant replacement at 5 p.m. I cycle back and forth along that route four times in a day. My bike spins along smoothly; my face has totally distracted me from any possible tyre problems.

Within a week of my implant being replaced, my spots start drying up. Buoyed by this, I decide to grab this moment to confront my other aches and pains, a full physical and emotional MOT. I ride my bike to the dentist where she takes X-rays and pokes around my mouth. When I am in her chair, I can feel the little metal instruments scratching at my molars and imagine every piece of contact is chipping away rotten bits of tooth. Recently, I've had dreams that my teeth are falling out, even though I brush them three times a day and floss after every meal, even in restaurants. It's become a nervous tic. My friends laugh at the habit. My mother scolds me for it, 'very vulgar,' she says. One man I briefly dated was so charmed by me flossing after consuming a packet of pub crisps, he called the barmaid over to take a look. 'Have you ever seen this?' he crowed. 'She's flossing in the bar!' The barmaid had a libertarian spirit. 'She can do what she wants,' she shrugged.

The flossing paid off: 'All good,' says the dentist, motioning for me to rinse.

On the way home, my bike doesn't feel so heavy and I smile as the wind whips past my face. I think about avoidance and how I tinker at the edges of problems, treating symptoms, not causes: sending postcards rather than making calls, pumping up tyres instead of wheeling my bike into a shop. A realisation begins to take shape about a pattern of historically outsourcing hard diagnostic work to the people around me; mostly lovers – always men. My friends believe I am hyper-independent but it is a messy independence, cobbled together. It reminds me of my terrible, patchwork attempts at sewing up holes in my clothes, which look fine from the outside but underneath are a tangle of crossed threads, bad stitching, barely holding the fabric together.

My ex was very good at sewing. He was good at lots of things: calling restaurants when I was too nervous to book reservations, getting me to go to the doctor and therapy and mending slow punctures. All my exes have been fixers who could look directly at my problems or pains without shying away from them. But I don't want to outsource my well-being anymore. How can you heal yourself if you don't allow a proper diagnosis of the injury in the first place?

When I get home from the dentist, I write a long letter to my stepdad because I need to stop avoiding his pain too, and the eventual loss that will come when he is not there to fix things for me. 'I haven't been very well,' I tell him. 'I hear you're thinking of stopping your medication? Is this true? Give me a ring and we can talk about it.'

When he calls me a few days later, I am walking to work because I have finally taken my bike to a local shop. I tell my stepdad about an art show I visited recently; he reports that he hasn't been able to get out in the garden lately. Then he references my letter, saying he's sorry I feel so hopeless about the economy, all these politicians are useless and always have been. 'When I die, I will leave you some money,' he says, which is partly him trying to fix things even after he is gone but is also a request for reassurance, because he can see his death is closer now than it ever has been before; he, like me, is scared. I take a deep breath. 'I will be very sad when you die,' I say. 'I'm going to come and see you soon.'

Cycling With Others

Just Who Is That Rider Coming Up Behind?

DAVID O'DOHERTY

The great thing about a career in stand-up comedy, I'd thought, was that it'd always be there. Sure, fewer people might come along as my clown car creaked over the hill, but if I could keep thinking of new jokes, *some*body would pay to sit in those seats. With respect to health practitioners everywhere, I alone could provide the best medicine.

Then came the spring of 2020 and laughter, or more accurately, the deadly mist of spume it bazooka-ed forth from your innards, officially became the worst medicine. Work slammed to a halt just as a romantic thing that had once shown great promise conked out. At a low ebb, and terrified at the prospect of the bat gloop getting into my eighty-something-year-old parents' crisp-bag lungs, I decided to accompany them out of the clammy lanes of Dublin City to my late grandmother's cottage 200 miles away, on the windy island of Achill – the last bit of Ireland before the tempestuous chowder of the Atlantic. 'Just for a couple of weeks,' Dad said, 'till everything's back to normal.'

Growing up, the only place we ever went on holidays was the cottage, but I didn't mind. The island was a wild playground: scream-swimming in the giant waves with my brother and sister; finding a dead shark that had been washed up on the rocks by the pirate castle; an ill-fated attempt to ride the ratty Achill bike that lived in the shed, up the mountain that ended with a chase from a ram and a square front wheel. There were always visitors – friends, cousins, neighbours – dinners for ten, loud boardgames, music, laughter. Now it was just us.

I don't recall the moment I decided to begin a part-for-part rebuild of Stephen Roche's 1987 Tour de France-winning bicycle, but my eBay Purchase History indicates that on 15 April, four weeks into my five months on Achill, I ordered a Campagnolo Corsa Record Mark II rear derailleur from a seller called Marko Tulio in Turin.

Despite stand-up comedy's late nights and chaotic festivals, I'd never realised how much structure it had brought to my life. For twenty years, I'd built my year around the Edinburgh Fringe, where I'd perform my latest show each day for the month of August. There were other annual landmarks – Bristol Comedy Garden in June, a night at London's Shepherd's Bush Empire in November. Sometimes in April I'd go to Melbourne for their comedy festival. I hadn't stopped to notice, but these beats had drummed the rhythm of my whole adult life.

Now there was a much bleaker daily pattern – the nightly news report of deaths and infections that my parents insisted on watching; tense trips to the supermarket as I tried to decipher Mum's list while maintaining distance from other uneasy shoppers. All the while, fixated on my main duty: defending the cottage-fortress from the apocalypse that appeared to be looming.

In the middle of this uncertainty, I retreated to my safest place, where I've always gone in times of crisis: old Youtube videos of my favourite sporting events. There's a comfort to watching these that I don't get from anything else. In an old movie or beloved series, I know there's a script and everyone is pretending. But in old sport clips, the agonised looks are real – these people are *actually* crying. There's even a phoney jeopardy that, despite having watched it ten times before, maybe I've misremembered the result? This is followed by genuine relief when it turns out exactly how I knew it was definitely going to.

IRELAND BEAT ENGLAND 1-0 EURO 1988 is a favourite. Yes, the result is in the title of the video, but can I still trust that it'll turn out that way again?

There are others: the British and Irish Lions rugby team's second test victory over South Africa in 1997; Katie Taylor's gold medal in boxing at the 2012 Olympics. Sure, it's all nonsense, with a weird patriotic twist for a not-at-all patriotic person but try telling that to my eyes as they fill with the delicious, salty tears of phoney triumph.

I thought the type of bicycle wheels Roche had used in '87 would be harder to source, the rim manu-facturer having gone out of business in the nineties. But, after a week, a pair appeared on one of the many vintage Italian bicycle parts Facebook groups I had joined. '€150!' I wrote in the comments, matching the asking price and hopefully sealing the deal. Seller Flavio soon slid into my direct messages, using a dialect of English I could soon identify as Google-translated from another language. 'It would give me infinite pleasure to provide these legendary wheels to a new family following your payment via PayPal.'

'Grazie Flavio!' I responded and forwarded the cash.

For all the criticism of the YouTube algorithm, at my lowest ebb in late March 2020, it served me up exactly what I needed. In the 'recommended for you' column, there began to appear episodes of Channel 4's nightly coverage of the 1987 Tour de France. These were full, wobbly VHS transfers of the half-hour show, complete with ad breaks for long-defunct lagers, cars that look twiggy-brittle by today's safety standards, and my favourite: impossibly dull, generic ads for things like lamb, bananas and cream.

At the time, Stephen Roche's unexpected victory in the three-and-a-half-week race was Ireland's greatest ever sporting triumph. Aside from some Nobel Prizes and Eurovisions, we'd never won much internationally. I remember being summoned to the sitting room by my mum and dad to watch the climax of an early stage. Roche – a Dubliner from just a few suburbs over – was unexpectedly rising up through the standings. But I was eleven years old and struggled to engage with the strange rhythm of this new sport.

Then it clicked. It was stage twenty-one, midway through the final week, and the riders were high in the Alps, when Roche, ignored by the TV cameras, launched a daring late attack that caught the race leader on the line.

'And just who is that rider coming up behind?' commentor Phil Liggett asks as a shape appears in the finishing straight. 'That looks like Roche ... THAT LOOKS LIKE STEPHEN ROCHE!' Roche collapses at the finish and is taken to hospital wearing an oxygen mask but recovers in time to cycle into Paris in the winner's yellow jersey a few days later. Twenty-four hours after that, I am one of one hundred thousand, tightly packed into Dublin's O'Connell Street to welcome our new hero home in his open-top bus.

Cycling became my obsession. I joined Roche's old club in Dublin and went on training rides some mornings before school. I'd borrow an Italian-English dictionary from the other end of the bookshop and attempt to translate my hero's latest exploits from the latest copy of the *Gazzetta dello Sport* until I was asked to leave. Whenever I passed his wife's boutique in Dublin city centre, I'd peek in through the manne-quins, on the off chance that he might have dropped in. I was definitely, 100 per cent, going to become the next Irish professional cyclist to win the Tour de France.

Unfortunately, my quest would be derailed by an almost complete lack of talent on my part, and the sport's implosion into a vortex of drugs scandals in the 1990s – this was even before the Lance Armstrong era. Put simply, many of my heroes had been cheating. It was a bitter break-up for me and I barely watched cycling for the next couple of decades. But for those few years around my early teens, I lived uncompli-catedly with the singular goal of becoming the next Stephen Roche.

I couldn't find a list of all the components that had been on Roche's bike, so I had to work it out from photographs. The saddle was obvious – a San Marco Rolls – but it was hard to read the name on the tyres. As for the chain, it was a complete guess. Most pros of the era used Sedis or Regina chains, and as Roche's Carrera team were from Italy, I opted for the Italian choice – the Regina CX. Seller Sergio described it in the listing as 'the Ferrari of the chain da bicicletta', and that was good enough for me.

After a few weeks on the island, our days had developed a familiar shape. I'd make breakfast while Dad looked at the previous day's paper and Mum read out bad news from the internet. In the afternoon, we'd sit outside as I chased more bike parts on my online groups, or I might go for a cycle on the ratty Achill bike that still lived in the shed.

The pain of being so far away from my old life was mitigated by knowing that the island was a good place to be stuck. There wasn't any FOMO to feel because the world had stopped – no MO to FO. We were doing OK and staying safe, and that was about as well as you could hope for.

Corsa Record is the last truly flamboyant set of brakes and gears from the gods of Italian bike components,

Campagnolo. The Japanese were coming, with their wind tunnels and lighter materials. Never again would aesthetics come before weight saving – never again would bicycles look so cool. The domed cover of Campagnolo's Delta brake calliper was like the roof of a palace, the urn-like sweep of the gear lever beckoned you to nudge it and go faster.

Each part had to be individually located and a price agreed with vendors in Poland, Belgium, Estonia, Hungary and Italy. By mid-May, I had made forty-three separate transactions. It took a lot of time, but then, I didn't have anything else to do. Also, I enjoyed the responses of the sellers when I explained the project I was undertaking:

BEST LUCK!

Wow cool plan stay safe.

Maybe now you will win 1987 Tour de France!!!

In May my aunt died, and I drove Dad back across the country to Dublin to attend a tiny memorial service. It was a silent journey, moving along eerily quiet roads, followed by the overwhelming stimulus of seeing people I loved again, albeit from a distance in the carpark of a crematorium. I left Dad with his brothers and sisters and called into my Dublin home to find that most of my houseplants had died. It didn't feel right to be there, so I grabbed the tools I'd need for the eventual bike assembly and left. I was happy when we got back to Mum on the island that night.

Soon the packages began to arrive at the cottage. At first Joe the postman would leave them on the gatepost and beep the horn of his post office van, but then I met him and explained the masterplan. Now he shared my obsession. 'Feels like a front derailleur,' he said one day, as he handed over the next brown packet. I looked shocked, till he admitted that it was written on the customs declaration.

Mum and Dad got into it too. 'We put all your bicycle bits into the recycling,' one of them would joke every couple of days. There is immense comfort in a recurring joke, particularly one that isn't funny the first time, but gradually Stockholms its way into your heart. They had a few. 'That must be the handlebars!' Mum would say as another small package containing a headset or bottom bracket arrived. Then feigning great wisdom, she'd add, 'You definitely shouldn't try to ride it till you've got the handlebars on.'

Some people never get past the eye-rolling relationship they had in their adolescence with their parents, cocksure that their emergence from these idiots has been a genetic fluke or cruel trick. And I could have been one of these people. But there we were, flung back together, twenty-something years after I'd moved out. I could appreciate them as the kind, weird housemates they were.

More than that, I could triangulate this branch of our family tree in real time and see which parts of me had been assembled from who. I had Mum's practicality, an understanding of what needed to be done and could be achieved on a given day. From Dad, I'd got my big, stupid ideas and a tendency to follow them most, if not all, of the way to resolution. Both were to blame for my sense of humour. And my love of sport. This is the best I can do by way of an explanation as to why, in April 2020, while the world stopped, I went through a second adolescence and attempted a part-for-part rebuild of Stephen Roche's 1987 Tour-de-France-winning bicycle.

The skeleton of any bicycle is the frame – the scaffold that everything hangs from. The now fifty-something other parts would be useless without the frame. In 1987, Roche's team rode frames built in the factory of former Tour of Italy winner Giovanni Battaglin, made from the lightest steel tubing of the day: Columbus SLX.

Battaglin frames would occasionally appear on the forums and groups that had become such a big part of my life, but they were always the wrong size. A six-foot mother and a five-foot-five father had begat a most unusually shaped son. I have short legs, but large feet and an incredibly long back. If you wanted to be nice, you could say I have a similar build to the footballer,

Lionel Messi. Less charitable friends have compared me to a panda or an Ewok.

I had accepted that a Battaglin of the correct era may not exist in my dimensions, and as this was a bicycle to be ridden, I was prepared to accept any frame made from Columbus SLX that fitted. The aim was to build a bike that *felt* like Roche's '87 machine. It didn't have to look exactly like it. I had set up various search alerts around the approximate sizes of 58 cm seat tube and 60 cm cross bar.

Then it happened. After six weeks of searching, a bike shop in Johannesburg listed a Battaglin frame in the 1987 Carrera team colours and in my size. I zoomed in on the picture and froze with excitement. Welded to the crossbar was a tiny piece of metal called a number hanger. A number hanger is where professional teams attach a rider's number in races like the Tour de France.

I requested a photo of the underside of the frame, where the serial number is stamped.

'Yes, my friend!' responded Alex Battaglin, son of Giovanni, when I forwarded the photo to the Battaglin factory, which is still in Marostica, Italy. 'It is 100 per cent real deal.' The frame was one of thirty the factory had built in the winter of 1986/87 for use by the Carrera cycling team in the following season.

Could it be Stephen Roche's frame? Rather than a tribute bike, could this be the very one I had watched him ride up La Plagne with Mum and Dad on 22 July 1987?

Well, no. Roche was 5'7", and would have ridden a smaller bike than this. But it was definitely a team-mate's bike, and that was close enough. Without another thought, I hit 'Buy it now' on the listing.

I'll skip over most of June – South Africa had entered a stringent lockdown and only essentials could be exported. I'd type in the tracking number most days to find it still sitting in the same corner of the same warehouse. Now there was a uselessness to my box of outdated bicycle parts, passively sitting there, as Mum or Dad did the recycling joke.

Late that month, the frame began to move. First to Durban, then to Amsterdam. It would be another couple of weeks before Joe the postman delivered it to the cottage.

'That must be the handlebars!' Mum remarked as he hauled the large box out of his van.

The construction took a couple of hours on the grass in the sunshine. I'd thought it through so many times that I already knew the precise order in which to add each freshly greased part. It fitted together perfectly – the brakes and gears barely required any adjustment. It felt like more of a reassembly than an assembly.

I pushed the bike down the stony driveway to the tarmac road, put one foot into the Campagnolo Corsa Record toe clip and glided off into the sun.

The main attraction of riding bikes, for me, is the effect it has on my brain. Perhaps because my body is taken up with the mechanics of it all: turning the pedals, watching the road, steering in the right direction – my mind is liberated. The greater the trust I have in a bike – one I've built myself and know won't fall apart – the freer my mind can be. I've thought of so many jokes while cycling and I've remembered things I'd long forgotten. I've had fleeting moments of the truest, most intense happiness.

As I rode my new bike on its maiden voyage up the hill by St Thomas's church and the old hotel, I thought of how Mum and Dad were safe in the cottage, and suddenly the pandemic and my heartbreak and the ashes of my career were a million miles away. I was fourteen years old again, the kid with the singular, uncomplicated goal. Turning those buttersmooth pedals on that perfect bike, in that instant, I had achieved it.

Life Cycles

JINI REDDY

I was seven when my family moved from London to a small village in Quebec. When we arrived, it was as though my life before this had been nothing but a dull blur. Now it burst into glorious colour, full of endless promise and beauty.

Those early days were bathed in wonder. There was now space and light, so much light – the bright, blazing Canadian sun, the wide blue skies, the white-tipped peaks of the Laurentian mountains and the jagged lightning forks that streaked across the sky on humid summer days. It was here, on a quiet rural street, that I learned to cycle. My first bike had banana handles and training wheels, but I soon shed the latter and began to discover my surroundings. This was a slice of countryside where you'd turn a corner and discover pretty chalets going up a not-yet-street.

I'd wobble along the muddy tracks littered with pebbles and rocks. Sometimes, I'd lose my balance and collect cuts and scrapes. I didn't care – I loved exploring and my parents didn't seem to mind my wandering off. I can still conjure the joy of grasping those handles, pedalling away from our house and feeling a surge of freedom.

In Montreal, an island city where my family eventually settled, I graduated to one of those bicycles with the curved, dropped handlebars. I had to lean down low to grasp them. I didn't love that bike – those handlebars were a pain – but all the kids had them. Sometimes I'd cycle to the corner shop (in Quebec this was known as the *depanneur*) for popsicles or candy. Other days the pull of a bike path along the mighty St Lawrence River drew me like a magnet, as did the intoxicating roar of the Lachine Rapids. I took the wild natural beauty of that landscape entirely for granted, and long after I'd left Canada, the path and the river took on the sheen of a paradise lost.

As a kid, cycling was also a way of gauging the pulse of my neighbourhood. I'd ride to the park and listlessly watch a game of softball, hoping one of the neighbourhood kids might put down their bat at the end, stroll over and say 'hi'. Sure, I had friends, but I was as geeky and bookish as they came, plus I was *ethnic*, a rarity in my very white neighbourhood. This meant eternally trying to blend in, while simultaneously wanting to be seen. On my bike though, I was a fleeting blur, which allowed me a degree of welcome invisibility; I felt entirely at ease. Sometimes I'd join a friend and we'd pedal round and round the wide, quiet streets, looking for action, or at least something out of the ordinary. If I was lucky, a boy I had a secret crush on might appear in his front yard, watering the grass or mowing the lawn. Then I'd feel a frisson of delight.

I took up tennis one summer when I was fourteen or fifteen and I'd cycle to and from the tennis club with my pals along the river path, racquet slung across my body in its cover, feeling good and fit and a little less nerdish and bookish. Life was getting exciting and I had dreams, so many dreams. Bikes didn't figure in them though.

After university, I left Canada, studied in France and then worked in London. To get around I walked or used the tube or buses. It never occurred to me to cycle. When I quit my job to travel in Nepal and India, I didn't want to be weighed down with bike panniers and a survival kit, spare tyres on unknown roads and reckless drivers. I couldn't even change a tyre. (I still can't.) And I shunned cycle gear – there would be no Lycra for me.

Then a few decades on, I found myself back in Quebec on a rented bicycle. This would be my first proper cycling trip. I was here on an assignment – I had become a travel writer by now – and I was tackling a Laurentian trail built on an old railway track. It was surrounded by lakes and forests and wound through the mountains, their soft green contours (for they were old), occasionally visible. Every kilometre of the trail was clearly numbered, as were the bed and breakfasts on it.

With no hills to struggle up, I was in heaven, and the journey, which lasted three or four days gave me a very intense and particular joy: the joy of motion and of exquisite freedom, the sweet rush of air on my face, and the deep satisfaction of making new discoveries entirely on my own steam. In this way, a journey on two wheels became a meditation and a dialogue between myself and whatever landscape I found myself in, something creative and fluid, a beautiful, safe cocoon.

I was so enamoured by all of this that as soon as I returned to my leafy London suburb, I went straight to a second-hand shop and bought my own bike. It was a silver mountain bike, and I still ride it. (Last year, a bike mechanic persuaded me to swap the chunky tyres for sleeker ones.) On it, I'd brave the roads to reach Wimbledon Common or just beyond it, Richmond Park. I'd carry snacks, a flask of tea for inclement weather, or cold water for balmy days when all that came into view took on a glorious lustre. I was content to cycle locally. I didn't enjoy lugging my bike onto trains to venture further afield and I feared the chaotic, traffic-clogged streets in the centre of town.

I revelled in my anonymity – a helmet is a wonderful, multi-tasking piece of armour. I liked being able to speed past people (particularly those who'd scowl if I 'dinged' my bell). Cycling was a kind of bliss and I was hungry for more. What I didn't anticipate was that my next adventure would end up being a blind date on two wheels.

I'd spent months arranging the trip, which would take me from Weymouth in Dorset on the South coast to St Malo in Brittany. It was a brand-new cross-Channel trail and I was going to be one of the first journalists to cycle the route. It was so new that it wasn't even fully signposted. I soon realised what I'd got myself into: ten days of huffing and puffing and 428 km to cover. Would my legs hold out, I wondered? What about the hills? I hated hills. And rain. I hated road cycling too. And my navigational skills were, to put it mildly, abysmal. Despite a degree in Geography,

I was hopeless at map reading, and GPS, which sounded terrifyingly technical to me, was still in its infancy.

It was decided that I'd be paired with a French cycling guide. He would be with me from Dorset all the way to Brittany. At least I'd not have to worry about getting lost. But this also meant hours of togetherness with a complete stranger. I thought of all those break-fasts, lunches and dinners – especially the breakfasts. I loathed speaking to people first thing in the morning. There'd be no more cycling in splendid solitude. What if we didn't get on? What if he – and early on, I was informed it was a 'he' – was a humourless bore? What if he thought I was tiresome? And what if I couldn't keep up with him? I was a slow cyclist, not some Tour de France Lycra-clad maniac. I fretted and rued the day I ever thought this was a good idea.

When the time came, I travelled down to Dorset by train. (God forbid I should add more cycling miles to the trip.) In Weymouth, I met the trip organisers. My guide would join us the following day in Wareham. He had crossed the Channel and at this very moment was cycling to Poole – doing the journey in reverse. I was given a 'brief' and shown maps I could barely read. Some days I'd be cycling 30 km, others a terrify-ing sounding 70 km, uphill.

My mind kept drifting to thoughts of my soon-to-be companion. In my mind's eye, he'd morphed into an anime of a crazed cycling professional with glazed eyes and a snarl. But when we finally met the following evening over dinner at our hotel – his name was Sebastien – all I could see was the worry in his eyes. He barely uttered a word. My guide, it dawned on me, was as anxious as I was. Possibly even more so. The tall, dark-haired, brown-eyed Frenchman warily spearing his fish and chips was as quiet as a mouse. Would I have to do all the talking on this trip? Mother him? He looked about a decade younger than me.

We were chaperoned, the organisers acting as bike escorts, as far as Studland Bay. There they waved us off. On the ferry across to Sandbanks, we were finally on our own. 'We will be in France soon,' said Sebastien, gazing out at the harbour, longingly, as he chained our bikes to the ferry. That evening, we made desultory small talk over a mediocre pub meal. The next morning, we left early for the ferry to Cherbourg. The minute we reached French soil, though, Sebastien was a man transformed, all traces of hesitation gone. He was on familiar ground. He walked taller, he even swapped his 'official guide' t-shirt, for a chic, white racing jacket.

'Follow me and you'll be fine. Allez!' he said confidently, as we cycled off the ferry and headed south of the city. Under grey skies, we pedalled past a sixteenth-century château with gardens and a moat, and then steadily and painfully uphill on country roads.

Over plates of lentil and sausage stew in a small café filled with stout, snowy-haired men – what must they make of us, I wondered? – he began to thaw. Sebastien told me he was from a Northern town, one he was fiercely proud of. He lived and breathed cycling. He was a besotted father of two small children. I, in turn, shared a bit about myself. I was far from the hard-bitten hack he'd imagined me to be.

Over the next few days, we cycled through marshland and valleys filled with orchids, forget-me-nots and foxgloves, and along rivers and granite cliffs. The skies changed, the sun came out and it stayed out. Sebastien was gentle and patient as I huffed and puffed, and he gave me a much-needed hug when I nearly cried at the end of a steep incline.

Over a late night drink in the town of Saint-Lô, known for its medieval church, he told me that his partner – yes, there was one – had asked him what he thought of me. 'Pas mal,' he'd said, eyeing me from behind his long, silky eyelashes. I smiled. I'd begun to think he wasn't bad either. Of course, I had no desire to dally with a man in a relationship. And yet and yet ... blame it on the lengthy Normandy lunches, the oysters, the apple tarts, the vichyssoise, the liberal doses of Calvados or the romantic, moonlit stroll back from Mont St-Michel when we'd parked the bikes at our auberge for a more leisurely visit, but somewhere along the way, the frisson turned to handholding and an illicit kiss. Just the one. OK, two.

I declined Sebastien's invitation to frolic in his *chambre*. I didn't want to, in truth and he didn't push it (perhaps he was relieved I'd said no). But the attraction transformed the trip into a heady, wonderful thing. We pedalled for long stretches without saying a word, and now the silence was an easy, companionable one. After a last meal of moules-frites en route to Saint-Malo, and unwilling to arrive at journey's end, we lingered over a flask of coffee on a windswept beach, both of us a little subdued.

That evening, we said our goodbyes. After a long hug, I checked into a poky hotel and Sebastien began the long ride back to his hometown. I wept, just a little, and then drowned my sorrows in a crêpe bretonne at a nearby bistro. A little after dawn the next morning, I made my way to the ferry which would take me back across the Channel. It felt strange to be alone, and I missed my guide terribly, but I also felt wonderfully alive. I'd lost weight and had never looked fitter. I'd also shaken off the residue of an old heartbreak and found my confidence again.

That summer, close to home, I raced around on my bike, lighter and happier than I had been in a long while. Of course, there would be other cycling adventures in the months and years to come – often day rides fitted into trips abroad. In a Rajasthani village, I borrowed a creaky two-wheeler and rode to a lake and watched the lumbering black buffalo wallow in the water; I once spent an afternoon cycling in the Jordanian desert, my body like coals in the heat. In a corner of coastal Spain, I cycled to a dazzling, wintry, flower-filled nature reserve, and in Zeeland in the south of Holland, a land where bikes are for everyone, including the disabled and elderly, I kept the sea in my sights and picnicked and pedalled to my heart's content.

Of course, punctuating it all was the pandemic, when my bike became my saviour and cycling my prayer. In the saddle, I got to know the back lanes of my neighbourhood, I'd cycle to the local cemetery and sit quietly on a bench in the outdoors, soak up the birdsong and revel in the safety of fresh air and solitude.

I'm now at the point in life where caring respon-sibilities for my elderly mother mean far-flung travel needs to be rationed and the future looms scarily. But cycling? It's one of my life's constants, it feeds my need for beauty, for delight and for aimless exploring. It makes my body hum and brings me safely back to the present. It has been my magic carpet and the catalyst for countless escapades. I hope to continue pedalling, nice and slowly, for the rest of my life, with the same curiosity that ignited my childhood.

My Horses!

YARA RODRIGUES FOWLER
& XANI BYRNE

—Tandem (Yara and Xani)

Portobello, Edinburgh.

The tandem leans against the fence, emerald and expectant in the February sun. The light picks out cobwebs and two scratches from the bike's last big cycle six months ago. It wears four red panniers, two custom bar bags, a friendly plastic windmill – our speedometer – and a phone holder.

This tandem has a past life. It was custom-made by bike-builder Andy Armour, as a declaration of love now passed. It's 531 steel and reassuringly heavy. S&S couplings mean its front and back halves can be easily separated and rejoined, allowing it to travel more comfortably on trains and in cars. Decorative lugs show colourful animals, love hearts, initials and the points of a compass. It has Rohloff hub gears, which, unusually, require both riders to stop pedalling for any gear change to happen. Finally, it has twin front disc brakes for motorbike-grade stopping power – essential for the weight of two people going downhill.

Technically, the front rider is called 'the pilot'. They have control of the steering, brakes and gears. On our ride, this will be Xani. The rear rider is known as 'the stoker'. They give up all notions of control. This will be Yara. Both riders have their own sets of handlebars, pedals and a seat. The two sets of pedals are connected to the cranks through a 'timing chain', which keeps the riders' legs moving in unison.

Communication and trust are essential.

—Stoker (Yara)

The weather is perfect: blue skies, no wind, 4 degrees. We're standing on a residential street a few hundred metres from the Firth of Forth, outside the house where Xani grew up. Karen, Xani's mum, is there and so is Beatrice, the mother of my best friend from school, Irene.

Just over two years ago, Alice, Xani's sister, died by suicide here in Portobello. Just over six years ago, Irene died by suicide in the Scottish Highlands.

Before she died, Xani had planned to ride the tandem with Alice to build her confidence cycling. Last summer, Xani cycled around the entire coast of the UK, each day with a different person bereaved by suicide. He called the project: Tandem Against Suicide.

Today we start our own, smaller tandem journey, 144 miles over two days from Edinburgh to North Shields, where me and Xani both live now with our respective partners, Mary and Andrew. Xani and Mary were the first new friends I made in the North-East. We put on our gloves and stand with a foot on either side of the bike.

Xani says, 'Right, we have to pedal at the same time—'

Karen says, 'Xani's got good at this bit, setting off with someone new.'

Left feet still on the ground, we position our right feet up on the pedals, ready to push.

Xani counts us down, 'Three, two, one – go!'

As we begin to move, Karen and Beatrice wave us off.

— *Tandem*

YARA

I can't control the
steering or the braking.
Or see what's in front
of us. The only thing
I have sole control over
is the bell.

I feel unnerved. But
we move leisurely along
the promenade, the Firth
of Forth opening up
to our left. In front of
me, Xani speaks in the
way that only a person
who has grown up
somewhere can – here
is the building that used
to be a pub, here are
the ramparts that were
broken in the storm.

The promenade
becomes a thin,
crumbling path, huge,
jagged rocks just below
us. I imagine all the

XANI

I can feel Yara's
uncertainty and try to
give her reassurance by
letting her know what's
coming up.

'Bump!'
'Bump!'
'Stop annnnd go!'

I take us along a
coastal 'path'. It's a
battered mash of patched
concrete repairs, jagged
rock and sand. The path
is narrow and we may
be stopped by the high
tide.

I think to myself,
'Concentrate! Avoid
slippy seaweed, change
grip, braking not
breaking. Annnd shift
weight back to balance,
rebalance. Cruise this bit
and pedal.'

ways we might crack our heads open.

I rationalise that at least Xani is in charge because he's the better cyclist and this, surely, will maximise our chances of survival.

Then, we approach our first incline, a modest few metres of paved cycle path through a sand dune. I look up at Xani's back as we reach the crest. It's like being on a roller coaster and I think about those kids who lost their legs at Alton Towers. I reach for non-existent brakes. Fucking terrified.

The path narrows with rocks on either side. We pass a smiling man with a small, sceptical dog.

Then sand covers the path and we decide to push. The weight of the bike leaves deep tyre tracks next to our footprints. It's heavy going for a few hundred metres. I stop and pick up a piece of sea-glass with safety wires inside it. Admiring the straight black lines inside the sea-softened edges.

—*Pilot (Xani)*

We cycle down the Scottish coast, high-tide, windless, a cool rising sun to the east. Past the new lagoons and out to Scotland's 'Golf Coast' – Archerfield, Gullane, North Berwick and thirty flat miles to Dunbar for lunch.

Brightly clad cycling clubs nod and smile from the other side of the road. Clicking cassettes announce more from behind.

'Hullo'

'Morning.'

'Hi.'

A small-coated boy at the side of the road cries, 'It's a *tandem*!'

I think of Alice as we pass the red sandstone gatehouse to Gosford House. A favourite place of hers, it's stuffed full of freemason symbolism and ornate sculpture; pyramid topped mausoleums within oval walled gardens surrounded by streams.

A sensibly dressed couple beam at us. The man shouts,

'She's not pedalling!'

They chuckle into their scarves, delighted at repeating the most frequent of tandem heckles. We smile. Sort of.

We slurp hot soup in Dunbar, then aim for Binning Memorial Wood.

Irene is here. Light shines through tall leafless beech trees. There are many stumps – downed by storm Arwen. I came with my mum a few years ago thinking of Alice.

We push the bike, walking side by side now, speaking of Irene and Alice. And then rhododendrons. And then death and how to remember people. Alice would've liked us talking like this, it's taken time.

Back on the road, I tell Yara about a game called, My Horses. It works like this: if you spot horses, you shout, 'My horses!' to claim them. Depictions of horses or unusual horses are worth extra points. If you see a cemetery, you shout, 'Bury your horses!' to reset the other person's tally to zero. We quickly become very competitive.

—*Tandem*

YARA

We spin and twist down
a hill towards the sea.
I duck my head to go
faster.

We hear the stream
before we see it, and
can't gauge the depth.

'Legs up!'

I lift my legs as high
as I can.

Xani has told me
about the hill out of
Pease Bay. It's the highest
hill in the journey. We
had agreed previously
that there'd be no
shame in getting off and
walking but nevertheless
I brace myself, anxious
about not being fit
enough and letting
Xani down.

We hold our feet
still as Xani changes

XANI

After Cove the road
dips towards the hidden
mobile homes of Pease
Bay. We lose seventy
metres over a mile and
quickly, very quickly,
pick up speed. The wind
pulls tears from my eyes
and I stay off the brakes.
I tuck and lift my body
to adjust the speed. I ask
how Yara's doing and
Wooop like a gull.

We slow before a
bend and then a flowing
river.

'Legs up!'

Feet-high and
splashing. A grinding
noise comes from the
disks.

The climb afterwards
is the hardest of the trip.
It's nearly 14 per cent

the gears. And then the climb begins.

It's not as hard as I thought it would be.

It's actually kind of easy.

Perhaps I am, in fact, a great cycling talent. Gifted by nature and weekly spin classes. Should I do the Tour de France?

I can hear Xani panting in front of me.

He moves the tandem in a zig zag shape up the road.

Evidence that I am not a great cycling talent: this is much easier than any hill I've ever climbed on a bike on my own. As we reach the peak, I feel humble and grateful to have Xani up front.

over 500 metres and water flows down the hill. There are high banks and hedges on either side of us.

I move the bike into bottom gear and grind it out.

Keep spinning, keep spinning.

I'm panting. Calves tight. No talking.

The road curves and although it's a short climb, it's longer than I remember. Yara's is quiet power from the back. She's not, by the sounds of it, out of breath. I need spin classes.

—*Stoker (Yara)*

We arrive in Berwick in the dark, half way through our two day journey. We dismount, my arse in disbelief, and carry the tandem up a set of curving steps on the stone embankment in front of the river Tweed. Liz, an artist in her sixties, opens the door. I've never met Liz, she's one of the many friends Xani made during his Tandem Against Suicide cycle around the UK.

Liz's top floor flat is everything I want. Central heating. Dinner in the oven. A big grey cat. Liz's art covers the walls. She fusses over us, pouring red wine and roasting stuffed aubergines. I flop onto the sofa.

Bob and Rita, who also live in the flat, join us for dinner. Bob and Rita have got together recently, having left long marriages with other people. Together, they have travelled the coast of Scotland, Bob photographing each river and Rita writing accompanying haikus. Bob tells us about his quest to photograph every historic county seat in the UK in alphabetical order. Rita tells us about her love for tall ships, and how she joined the crew of a (not tall) ship travelling from England to Australia, alone with thirteen seamen.

Liz, Bob, and Rita have been friends for over thirty years. They move around each other with care and ease. Liz tells me that her best friend died by suicide a few years ago. Rita's brother died by suicide when she was fifteen. We talk about suicide prevention, what has changed and what has stayed the same.

And then Rita mentions her harp, which she plays while reading her poetry.

'I built it myself with the help of a German instructor. I dyed it pink and carved a horse's head into the crown.'

Rita shows us a photo.

Later, as we settle, exhausted, into our twin beds, I say,

'Liz's harp.'

'Yeah?'

'That's my horse.'

—*Pilot (Xani)*

I wake first. I pull the Blu Tack I use as earplugs from each ear and listen to the dawn chorus,

KREEEE! Huuueeep! Pip. Pip. HA-ha-ha!

Birds fly so close I can hear the swoops, thuds, landings and tapping of feet.

I go downstairs to a kitchen sunrise. The wall glows for five minutes – Liz talks about an intergenerational Sunday community repair shop – and then settles, white.

We mount the bike.

'Ready?'

'Ready.'

Right feet high.

'Three, two, one aaannnnd – go!'

We wave goodbye to Liz, Bob and Rita. Bob photographs us as we pedal along the Berwick walls towards the bridge. With Eyemouth and Burnouth behind us, we're at the third mouth: Tweedmouth.

My arse has the sharp pain of emerging saddle sores. Yara tells me that I'm shifting in my seat more than yesterday. Yup. I carefully adjust myself into the disappointing padding.

We climb sharply up to an off-road cliff-top path. Mud, and deep rutted tracks. The unfenced thirty-foot drop only a few metres to our left reminds me of those who've stood on the edge and looked out. Below us, waves crash into the shore in clean straight lines.

The vertical lines of Holy Island and Bamburgh Castle break up the horizon; they watch us and wonder when we'll arrive. Optimistically, Google Maps says we are two hours away.

Twenty-eight-inch tyres and low gears keep us moving through the mud. It clumps and catches where it can. Dirty wool gathers on barbed wire and the gates between fields punctuate our conversation. They give us our rhythm for the day. I slow down, Yara hops off, hauls open a gate and I trundle the tandem through. The gate clanks closed, and Yara gets back on

Right foot high.

'Three, two, one – go!'

'My horses!'

—*Tandem (Yara and Xani)*

The signs near Craster offer a shortcut along a road but we refuse it, preferring to stick to the coastal route. We immediately bump into a friend of a friend from North Shields with her two siblings, smiling and muddy.

The path takes us down a wet muddy slope. The ground here is the wettest we've come across so far.

'When we fall, fall left.'

We fall left.

'One, two, three—'

We move down and across the path.

We fall left.

'One, two, three—'

We move down and across the path.

Somehow, with no hesitation and entirely together, we fall right. At the end of the hill Howick Burn flows into the sea by an opening of tall trees. It is high tide. Curlews congregate chirping and picking through masses of entangled seaweed. The last stretch down the Northumberland coast is so long. Our bums hurt. Every beach is gorgeous.

In Amble, we buy Lucozade. We drink the Lucozade. We pass two fields of horses and a poster of a missing pony. We cycle alongside the A1 and get temporarily lost.

'One, two, three—'

It is dark and we stop opposite a shopping complex to don more reflective gear. This is Blyth, finally. We call Mary, who has promised dinner, letting her know we're 'a long hour away'. Because tandems defy algorithmic prediction of time – we're faster on the downhills and slower on the uphills – our speed unknown until it happens.

The streets around us become suburban. We stop and start for cars. A group of teenage boys bunch together in the street ahead of us and we brace ourselves for mockery.

'Sick bike!'

We pull into Blyth beach car park, passing bemused couples steaming up windscreens with fish and chips. Vinegar smell. We've disappointed Google Maps but don't check anymore. This is home territory. We take the unlit path through the dunes. Smooth tarmac with a gentle breeze behind us. Swishing long grasses. Our lights reveal only a few metres ahead.

The windmill spins and squeaks on the handlebars. There's no one else on the twisting path in the dark. The riding is intuitive. Yara anticipates turns, hills and cruising. Our legs feel like burnt-out sofas left in the rain.

The welcoming moon peeks through the clouds. Gradually then suddenly lighting the sea and path ahead.

Seaton Sluice. Old Hartley. Whitley Bay. St Mary's lighthouse doesn't wink but the lights of Spanish City tell us we're almost home. Past the 'Jesus Saves' sign, past Yara and Andrew's house, and the red lettering of The Grand Hotel. A final slow, steady climb to finish.

We dismount, our bodies stiff yet somehow also floating. The door to Mary and Xani's house is unlocked and, as we open it, there is a moment when we see Mary and Andrew, surrounded by warmth and the smell of dinner, and they are waiting for us, although we have already arrived.

And then the four of us fill the corridor. Removing shoes and gloves and receiving hugs and kisses.

We eat big bowls of orzo with vegetables and then flapjacks straight from the oven. We stroke the cat. Andrew and Mary ask us questions that we won't remember. We take a sofa each, slowly curling into the shape of commas.

Roz

DERVLA MURPHY

Dunkirk to Teheran

I had planned a route to India through France, Italy, Yugoslavia, Bulgaria, Turkey, Persia, Afghanistan and Pakistan. Departure Day was to have been 7 January 1963, but by then the freak weather of that year had reached even Ireland and I postponed 'D-Day' for a week, innocently supposing that these conditions 'could not go on'. But of course they did go on, and in my impatience to be off I decided that to postpone departure from week to week would not be practical – though in retrospect I realised that it would have been a lot more practical than heading for Central Europe during the coldest winter in eighty years.

I shall never forget that dark ice-bound morning when I began to cycle east from Dunkirk; to have the fulfilment of a twenty-one-year-old ambition apparently within one's grasp can be quite disconcerting. This was a moment I had thought about so often that when I actually found myself living through it I felt as though some favourite scene from a novel had come, incredibly, to life. However, within a few weeks my journey had degenerated from a happy-go-lucky cycle trek to a grim struggle for progress by *any* means along roads long lost beneath snow and ice.

At first my disappointment was acute, but I had set out to enjoy myself by seeing the world, not to make or break any record, so I soon became adjusted to these conditions, which led to quite a few interesting adventures. Also, I was aware of 'seeing the world' in circumstances unique to my generation. Should I survive to the end of this century it will be impressive to recall that I crossed the breadth of Europe in the winter of 1963, when every humdrum detail of daily life was made tensely dramatic by the weather and going shopping became a scaled-down Expedition to the Antarctic. It was neat hell at the time – I cycled up to the Rouen Youth Hostel with a quarter-inch icicle firmly attached to my nose and more than once the agony of frozen fingers made me weep rather uncharacteristically – yet it seemed a reasonably good exchange for the satisfaction of cycling all the way to India.

I give full marks to Italy for the superb efficiency with which her main northern roads were kept clear during that January. Having been compelled to take a train from Grenoble to Turin, across the Alps, I found myself able to cycle, and enjoy it, almost all the way to Nova Gorizia, through a deserted and impeccably beautiful Venice.

At this bisected frontier town of Nova Gorizia the formalities for being admitted into Yugoslavia seemed diabolically complicated. Repeatedly I was shuttled back and forth through the darkness from Police to Customs Officers; then, while innumerable forms were being completed in triplicate, I stood shivering outside warm offices, trying to explain why I was so improbably entering Yugoslavia with a bicycle on 28 January. And every time I took off a glove to sign yet another document the bitter wind seared my hand like caustic acid.

Suddenly a policeman shouted to someone in another room and a tall, rugged-featured woman, wearing Customs Officer's uniform, appeared beside me. I stared at her in horror, only then remembering that my automatic lay in the right-hand pocket of my slacks, where the most casual search would at once detect a sinister hard object. In the stress and strain of searching Gorizia for the open frontier post (there were four in all, but three were closed to tourists) I had quite forgotten my ingenious scheme for concealing the weapon. So now I foresaw myself being hurled into the nearest dungeon, from which I would eventually emerge, emaciated and broken in spirit, after years of negotiations between two governments who are not, diplomatically, on speaking terms. But alarm was unnecessary. The formidable female took one quick look at my intricately laden bicycle, my knapsack with its protruding loaf of bread and my scruffy self. Then she burst into good-humoured laughter – of which one would not have believed her capable – slapped me on the back and waved me towards the frontier. It was 6.15 p.m. when I passed under the railway bridge with 'Jugoslavija' painted across it in huge letters.

Two miles from the frontier, having cycled along an unlighted road that leads away from Italy and then curves back, I came to Nova Gorica, the Yugoslav half of the town. Here, beneath the weak glow of a street lamp, a solitary figure was walking ahead of me. Overtaking it I saw a good-looking girl who, in reply to my questions, said, 'Yes' she spoke German, but 'No' there wasn't a cheap inn available, only the Tourist Hotel, which was very expensive. Even in the dim light my look of dismay must have been apparent, because she immediately added an invitation to come home with her for the night. As this was within my first hour of entering Slovenia I was astonished; but soon I learnt that such kindness is common form in that region.

While we walked between high blocks of workers' flats, Romana told me that she shared a room with two other typists employed in a local factory at £3 per week, but as one was away in hospital there would be plenty of space for me.

The little room, at the top of three flights of stairs, was clean and adequately furnished, though the only means of cooking was an electric ring, and the bathroom and lavatory were shared with three families living, in one room each, on the same floor. Arita, Romana's roommate, gave me a most enthusiastic welcome and we settled down to a meal of very curious soup, concocted out of some anaemic meat broth, in which lightly whipped eggs were cooked, followed by my bread and cheese (imported from Italy) and coffee (imported from Ireland).

I found these youngsters delightful company – vivacious, perfectly mannered and intelligent. They were simply dressed and it was pleasant to see their clear-skinned faces, innocent of any make-up, and their well-groomed heads of unpermed sanely-cut hair. I noted too the impressive row of books in the little shelf by the stove – among them translations of

Dubliners, The Heart of the Matter, The Coiners, Black and Red and *The Leopard*.

Anticipating a tough mountain ride on the following day I was relieved to find that 9.30 p.m. was bedtime, as these girls rise at 5.30 a.m. to catch the factory bus and be at work by seven o'clock.

It was a deceptively fine morning when I left Nova Gorica. The second-class but well-kept road to Ljubljana wound through a range of fissured mountains, whose lower slopes were studded with tiny villages of brown-roofed, ramshackle farmhouses, and whose upper slopes, of perpendicular bare rock, gave the valley an odd appearance, as though it had been artificially walled in from the rest of the world. Then, towards midday, as I was revelling in the still, crisp air and brilliant sunshine, a violent wind arose. Whether because of the peculiar configuration of the mountains here, or because it was one more manifestation of freakish weather, this wind blew with a force such as I had never previously encountered. Before I could adjust myself on the saddle to do battle with my new enemy it had lifted me right off Roz and deposited me on a heap of gravel by the wayside. None the worse, I remounted, but ten minutes later, despite my efforts to hold Roz on the road and myself on Roz, we were again separated, and this time I went rolling down a fifteen-foot sloping ditch, unable to get a grip on the icy bank to check my fall. I ended up on a stream which happily was frozen so solid that my impact produced not a crack in the ice. After crawling cautiously along the stream for some twenty yards, to find a way up to the road and Roz, I decided that from now on walking was the only logical means of progress.

At the valley's end my road started to climb the mountains, sweeping up and up and again up, in a series of hairpin bends that each revealed a view more wild and splendid than the last. At one such bend I was actually frightened by the power of the gale; I couldn't walk against it, and for some four or five minutes I simply stood, bent over Roz, my body braced with all its strength in the effort to hold us both on the road.

Near the top of the pass, seven miles from the valley floor, things were further complicated by the reappearance of my old enemies – packed snow and black ice underfoot. On the west side of this mountain range there had been strangely little snow (although everything that could freeze had frozen) but now, going over the pass, I was abruptly back to the too-familiar vision of a landscape completely white, each contour and angle rounded and disguised. Then yet another blizzard started, the flakes whirling round me like a host of malicious little white demons.

By now I was exhausted from the struggle uphill against the gale and the agony of frost-bitten hands and feet. My hands were too numb for me to consult the map, which in any case would probably have been ripped away by the wind or rendered illegible by the snow. Crawling along over the ice, I told myself that this was an advantage, because if no village was marked I would probably curl up by the wayside in despair.

In fact there was a tiny village, called Hŕusevje, less than two miles ahead, and on arriving there I thanked my guardian angel, as I blundered about among piles of snow stacked four and five feet high on either side of the road, searching for something that looked like an inn. At last I saw two old men emerging from a doorway, wiping their moustaches with the backs of their hands. This looked hopeful, so I dragged Roz over a pile of snow, propped her against the wall, and entered the two-storeyed stone house.

Obviously the primary need was brandy, yet my face was so numb that I couldn't articulate one word. I merely pointed to the relevant bottle, and stood by the stove to thaw out, while a group of card-playing men stared at me with a trace of that hostility shown by all peasants in remote places to unexpected strangers. Then an old man came rushing in to inform the company that I had arrived with a bicycle – and, as I soon recovered the power of speech, friendly relations were easily established.

I now broached the subject of accommodation for the night and the landlady at once broke into excited discussions with her customers. In the middle of this the door opened again and a young woman entered. She was hailed with great relief all round, and turning to me introduced herself in English as a local social worker. She explained that tourists are not allowed to stay in any but Tourist Hotels – which meant yet another disruption of my plans, for I had intended, on crossing the frontier from expensive Italy, to settle down in some village such as Hŕusevje and wait there, living cheaply, until weather conditions again permitted cycling.

However, *pace* Government regulations, it was obvious that this particular tourist could not now be accommodated anywhere but at the village inn. The next step was to contact the local policeman, so that he might give his blessing to the irregularity. This formality completed, I was shown up to my large room, which contained one small bed in a corner and nothing else whatever.

When I came down to eat some bread and cheese by the stove in the pub I found a young girl waiting for me – one who was to prove a true friend and who provided me with the most congenial companionship during the following days. A daughter of the local postman and postwoman, Irena was a student of psychology at Ljubljana University, and was now home for the winter vacation, that is to say, the month of January. She was due to return to Ljubljana on 31 January, and she advised me to wait at Hfusevje until then, as the road down to the plain would be impassable after such a blizzard. She added that she would smuggle me into her room at the University Students' Hostel, where one of the five beds was vacant, thus saving me the expense of the Tourist Hotel.

For the next two days my landlady mothered me so successfully that I settled down to write as happily as though I were in my own home. Indeed, I was enthusiastically adopted by the whole locality; the men reported my arrival to their womenfolk who paid a special call at the inn to shake me by the hand, slap me on the back, tell me that I was welcome to Slovenia, and, as often as not, invite me to come and stay in their homes indefinitely.

On the 31st Roz and I left for Ljubljana in a snow-chained truck and that drive was one of the worst frustrations of the expedition. The road swept down for thirty miles through magnificent mountains and valleys and pine forests, all glittering in the sunshine as though covered in diamond-dust, yet here was I being ignominiously transported by truck. However, I could not complain of having no time to admire my surroundings, for the ice was so treacherous that it took us three hours to cover forty-five miles.

The university hostel, converted from an old convent, was such a vast building that there was little difficulty in smuggling me to Irena's room. Personally I was of the opinion that the Authorities, who had given me a warm welcome when I arrived in search of Irena, were perfectly well aware of the situation and quite happy about it, but my roommates were obviously enjoying the conspiracy so I entered into the spirit of the thing with as much enthusiasm as my more advanced years allowed.

On the following morning Roz and I left Irena and her companions in Ljubljana, equipped with a bundle of introductions from them to Slovenes living all along our route, but after cycling about twenty miles we were again forced to get a lift by truck to Zagreb.

'Roz' is an extract from *Full Tilt: Ireland to India with a Bicycle* (London: Eland Books, 1965)

About the Contributors

Imogen Binnie is the author of the novel *Nevada*, which won the Betty Berzon Emerging Writer Award and was a finalist for the 2014 Lambda Literary Award for Transgender Fiction. A writer for several television shows and a former columnist for *Maximum Rocknroll*, she lives in Vermont with her family.

Xani Byrne is a cyclist from Edinburgh. He is an Educational Psychologist and Trainee Clinical Psychologist working in the NHS. Xani's 'Tandem Against Suicide' project received a Prime Minister's Points of Light award in 2023 for a fundraising cycle around the coast of Great Britain with families bereaved by suicide.

Aniefiok 'Neef' Ekpoudom is a writer from South London who documents and explores culture in contemporary Britain. In his work, Aniefiok tells stories about the people, voices and communities shaping the country as it exists today. His first book, *Where We Come From: Rap, Home & Hope in Modern Britain*, is a narrative driven social history of British Rap, spanning from the 60s to present day. It was released by Faber & Faber in January 2024. He writes for the *Guardian*, *British GQ*, *Vogue* and more. Elsewhere he works on creative projects with Google, GRM Daily, Nike, Netflix, adidas and more. He is a recipient of a British Journalism Award's and was named on the Forbes 30 Under 30 List in Media & Marketing.

Yara Rodrigues Fowler is from South London. Her first novel, *Stubborn Archivist,* was published in 2019 and longlisted for the Dylan Thomas Prize and the Desmond Elliot Prize, and Yara was shortlisted for the Sunday Times Young Writer of the Year 2019. Yara's second novel, *there are more things*, was published in 2022 and nominated for the Orwell Prize for Political Fiction and Goldsmiths Prize. It was one of the *Sunday Times*, BBC Culture and *New Statesman*'s books of the Year. In 2023, Yara was chosen as one of *Granta*'s 'Best Young British Novelists' in their once-a-decade list.

Mina Holland is a writer, editor and storyteller. Until recently, she split her time between the *Guardian*, where she was an editor on the Feast team, and writing about matters of food, drink and lifestyle for other publications and brands, such as Noble Rot and TOAST. She is the author *The Edible Atlas: Around the World in 39 Cuisines* and *Mamma: Reflections On The Food That Makes Us*. She lives in London and her memoir, *Lifeblood*, publishes in 2025 via Daunt Books.

Annie Lord grew up in Otley, a town on the outskirts of Leeds. She writes *Vogue*'s dating column and her first book, *Notes on Heartbreak*, was published in 2022.

Moya Lothian-McLean is a politics and culture writer.

Jon McGregor is the author of five novels and two story collections. He is Professor of Creative Writing at the University of Nottingham, where he edits the Letters Page, a literary journal in letters. He was born in Bermuda, grew up in Norfolk, and now lives in Nottingham.

Dervla Murphy's first book, *Full Tilt: Ireland to India with a Bicycle*, was published in 1965. Over twenty other titles followed. Dervla won worldwide praise for her writing and was often described as a 'travel legend' and 'the first lady of Irish cycling'. She continued to travel around the world and remained passionate about politics, conservation, bicycling and beer, well into her eighties.

David O'Doherty is a comedian and children's author from Dublin, as well as a former recipient of the Perrier Award for Most Outstanding Show at The Edinburgh Fringe. He has appeared on TV programmes such as *QI*, *Would I Lie To You?* and *Conan O'Brien*. His last book for kids, *The Summer I Robbed a Bank*, won Children's Book of the Year at the Irish Book Awards. He used to work in a bike shop and is reputed to own nineteen bikes.

Jini Reddy is an author and journalist whose writing has appeared in the *Guardian*, *The Times*, *TIME*, *i-paper*, *Financial Times*, *National Geographic* and many other publications. Her most recent book, *Wanderland*, was shortlisted for the Stanford Dolman Travel Book of the Year Award and for the Wainwright Prize. Her first, *Wild Times*, was awarded the British Guild of Travel Writers Adele Evans Award. She has contributed to anthologies, including the landmark *Women on Nature*. In 2019, she was named one of *National Geographic's* Women of Impact. Born in London to Indian parents from South Africa, Jini grew up in Montreal, and currently lives in leafy Wimbledon.

Ashleigh Young is the author of the award-winning essay collection, *Can You Tolerate This?*, as well as two critically acclaimed books of poetry, *Magnificent Moon* and *How I Get Ready*. Young is the recipient of a 2017 Windham Campbell Prize in Nonfiction and an Ockham Award, among other honours, and is an editor at Te Herenga Waka University Press in Wellington.

Daunt Books

Founded in 2010, Daunt Books Publishing grew out of Daunt Books, independent booksellers with shops in London and the south of England. We publish the finest writing in English and in translation, from literary fiction – novels and short stories – to narrative non-fiction, including essays and memoirs. Our modern classics list revives authors whose work has unjustly fallen out of print. In 2020 we launched Daunt Books Originals, an imprint for bold and inventive new writing.

www.dauntbookspublishing.co.uk